I0817880

# *TIMELESS DESTINY*

First Edition, December 2023



Vecteezy.com

## Novels By Bernard Cenney:

SPARROW'S TEARS

CLOSE YOUR EYES AND SEE

TIMELESS TERROR

TIMELESS SOLDIER

TIMELESS EMBRACE

TIMELESS DESTINY

# *TIMELESS DESTINY*
# BERNARD CENNEY

## AUTHOR'S NOTE:

This literary manuscript is entirely a work of fiction. Any similarity or resemblance to businesses, organizations, places, names, characters, real persons, incidents, or events is purely coincidental, unintentional, imaginary, or used in a fictitious manner.

**IN MEMORIAM:**

JAMES B. CENNEY
19 OCT 1989 — 11 OCT 2004

LOVED FOREVER

Send your tax deductible contributions to find a cure for children's hypertrophic cardiomyopathy to:

www.childrenscardiomyopathy.org

Thank you.
Bernard Cenney

# DEDICATION:

Special thanks go to my wife, Kongsri Cenney.

Over thirty-seven years ago in Southeast Asia, Kongsri left her family, her country, and everything that was familiar to her in order to marry a young American Special Forces Captain. She took my hand and never looked back. We have supported each other in conflict and peace, hardship and success, sorrow and joy. Through it all she has loved me unconditionally and never left my side.

Bernard Cenney
Lt. Colonel (Retired)
United States Army
8 January 2024

# *PREFACE*

*Perhaps someone who is mourning will find solace in the following.*

The worst experience to suffer is the death of your child.

The hypertrophic cardiomyopathy death of my fourteen-year-old son, James Cenney, was a tragedy that nothing in this present world can ever make right. James was young, innocent, and just starting life. One day he was playing his guitar; the next day he was not. One day he was playing football and exercising; the next day he was not. One day he was going to school, laughing, and joking; the next day he was not. One day he was here — the next day he was gone. No father should outlive his child.

James' unexpected death shattered my wife, my daughters, and me. Parents who lose their child never bounce back. Speaking for myself, his death eroded my spirit, my resiliency, my resolve, my fortitude, my joy, my hope, and my self-worth. It became impossible to feel any sort of happiness for years.

The sheer madness and incomprehensible horror of his death destroyed my understanding of a loving God. Suffering became a daily companion. I convulsed at the clichés of "all things happen for a reason," or "God never gives us any burden we can't handle." I avoided those who declared they were "blessed by God." It made me feel as if my life was surely cursed by him.

I had seen death before, privately and in my military career. But this was intensely more personal, more visceral, more agonizing. Surely God did not want this to happen; surely God was mourning just as we were; surely God was in despair over this tragedy; surely God — as my father — empathized.

I started to have vivid dreams and visions of James. I documented and kept a record of them all. I could never (and still can't) control the mental image of my son James passing away. I have always (and still do) blame myself for not being able to somehow save him. It became an unimaginable situation. It began replaying itself, over and over, every day of my life. I was in a very dark place.

The military community at Fort Sam Houston provided us with overwhelming support. Group and individual therapy was helpful at first, but soon was not enough for me. Depression developed into apathy to even want to wake up. A terrible schism evolved between wishing for nonexistence, and a father's obligations to the rest of his family.

I just couldn't believe that James had passed away. Sometimes I think he will walk through the door, and everything will be as it once was. After he died, I thought the world would end. In my mind, I waited for the end to come. But it didn't. People went to work, children went to school, and life kept grinding on. My mind tore to pieces over whether to stop moving or to keep pushing onward.

My wife and daughters were suffering terribly as well, perhaps even more than me. Together as a family, we comforted and supported each other. I don't believe it would have been possible for me to move on without the love of my family. I felt that I had to show strength for them. I had to be the father to push everyone onward and hold the family together. If I gave up, I would have failed everyone. I knew that I had to control my grief and move forever onward. These were the thoughts constantly pounding through my mind.

James' death started me to think deeply, perhaps for the first time in my life, and to read incessantly. I read *The Upanishads*, *The Tibetan Book of the Dead*, and *The Bible*. I studied the Greek historians and philosophers: Aeschylus, Aristotle, Epictetus, Herodotus, Plato, and Sophocles. I read works by Billy Graham, Dalai Lama, Deepak Chopra, Dr. Melvin Morse, and Dr. Raymond Moody, to name just a few. I devoured just about any book that dealt with the subject of reincarnation and life after death. *The New Testament* was the enlightened example to me that life is suffering, and you must force yourself through the pain and move forward.

Pain and suffering must be understood and fully absorbed. You cannot deaden the feelings. You cannot even attempt to understand life without suffering. The message I gleaned from *The Gospel of John* brought hope to me. Sometimes a spiritual transcendence can occur from experiencing intense sorrow.

What I understood for myself was disconcerting. Tragedy strikes everyone. Those who think they are immune, only have but to wait. It will come. More tragedy is lingering around the corner. Life is the great equalizer. You cannot barter for a better life. You must push on through tragedy with all the strength you have inside. Despite unanswered prayers, you must forever move forward and do what's right. To be alive is to have constant pain and struggle.

You must push yourself forward. You must pray. You must master discipline. You must keep focus. You must practice compassion. You must hone understanding. You must think. Learn to speak less, and listen more. Put others first and yourself second. Try to help as many people as you can in your life, and if you can't help them at least don't hurt them. The best possible life you can have is one of helping others, and constantly striving to do what is right, regardless of the outcome.

How do you know what is right? Search your heart. Buddha is about compassion; Jesus is about love. Put those together and it's pretty powerful. Treat everyone with dignity, respect, love, and compassion. The reward you receive is the knowledge and peace of mind that you did what was right.

I spent a career in the US Army continually taking and giving orders, and telling soldiers what to do. I came to an understanding that I could not control events. All I could do was try to lead a good life, help others, and set a positive example. I have failed over and over again. My joy comes from helping others when I can, and watching my children excel and lead good lives.

Now to the subject of my novels.

Writing the books *Sparrow's Tears, Close Your Eyes and See, Timeless Terror, Timeless Soldier, Timeless Embrace,* and *Timeless Destiny* became therapy for me — the best therapy. When I think of my son James, I see him always helping others — those who could not help themselves — whether at home or in school. He made me realize that nothing is without purpose; that there is a majestic plan which unfolds itself across the vastness of time equally embracing each life, no more or less important than another. Writing the novels became my way of honoring and paying tribute to James. It allowed me to envision him as an adult, giving him the type of life I would have wished for him. Writing the books allowed me to dream my son a life which I felt had ended too quickly. James Cenney is alive in the pages of my novels. He encourages my readers and me to move forever forward in life.

The hero of my novels — Captain James Ross — is patterned after my son. They both have the same looks, style, loves, and ambience. They are both heroes. But even more than that, as my son James Cenney would say, they "… are intelligent human beings."

My fervent hope is that veterans who are suffering from PTSD and depression can use fiction writing as therapy.

Bernard Cenney
Floresville, Texas

# *TIMELESS DESTINY*

# *PART ONE*

*The soldiers also mocked him, and taking sour wine offered it to him to drink, and said to him, If thou art King of the Jews deliver thyself. Then Longinus, a certain soldier, taking a spear, pierced his side, and presently there came forth blood and water.*

Nicodemus
33 AD
Pharisee

# *PROLOGUE*

## *SKULL PLACE 33 AD*

The hour was three on Friday afternoon.

The Centurian surveyed the scene and thought to himself.

*Why am I here?*

*Why am I sitting here, watching this insanity?*

*This terrible, this macabre travesty of justice.*

*Is this what it comes down to, my life?*

*Just being an instrument of a deranged empire?*

*An empire that is for sale at every level?*

*For sale by corrupt politicians who jail their opponents and rule by peddling their influence?*

The Centurian was troubled.

*My Legionnaires are tired.*

*They long to be home.*

*I long to be home.*

*I miss my wife, my children, and all the sweetness that is Rome.*

But the Centurian was not home. On this most dreary and desolate of days, he found himself in the Judaea District just outside of Jerusalem. He was at a spot the locals called "Golgotha," meaning "skull place" in Aramaic.

He thought, *How did I end up here at this forsaken place?*

He allowed himself the luxury to remember, to reflect back.

Longinus had been one of those patriotic youths who had sat on his father's knee and listened intently to his stories of past glories as a Legionnaire. The stories enthralled and thrilled him as a child. So, when Longinus himself turned seventeen he joined up. Rome had dominated the world for the past 300 years, and he wanted to be a part of it. He had been a Legionnaire now for the past seventeen years, and a Centurian for six of those. His military skills had been tested during many campaigns — the Pannonian, the Arminius, and the Germanic. His left forearm bore the mark of Rome — SPQR — Senatus Populusque Romanus.

*I sacrificed for Rome.*

*I killed for Rome.*

*I bled for Rome.*

And now Longinus found himself 4000 kilometers from Rome.

*I've been exiled to this God forsaken place.*

Longinus was in Jerusalem with a hundred Legionnaires to carry out Rome's supreme capital punishment for insurrection — a crucifixion. This particular crucifixion was a long time in coming. For the past year the Sadducees and Pharisees had been pushing for it. These so called "Holy Men" were nothing more than wealthy upper-class priests whose personal corruption knew no bounds.

*And who was this treacherous man ... this treasonous insurrectionist that had so heinously angered the High Priest of Jerusalem, one Joseph Caiaphas?*

*A carpenter from Nazareth, that's who.*

*A carpenter!*

Longinus raised his fist to Jupiter.

*By the Gods this was insanity!*

"Father forgive them, for they know not what they do," said Jesus.

*Forgive them? How can the man say that? Why would he say that? How can he forgive us for torturing him, for murdering him? This Jesus — this Jesus of Nazareth was a simple man, a man who actually told people to "love your enemies."*

*Love your enemies?*

*I've lost track of how many enemies I have.*

But the Sadducees and Pharisees were intent on killing Jesus. They'd had enough of the rabble-rousing Nazarene — the carpenter who was preaching love to the people. The man had thousands of followers. A message had to be sent to them. The last straw was when Jesus entered the temple, the most holy of holies, and overturned the money changers tables, showing utter contempt for the temple priests and their corrupt influence peddling schemes. Then this week he actually rode on a donkey into Jerusalem mimicking King Solomon's riding of a donkey on the day he became the new King of Israel. The Sadducees and Pharisees could stand no more. Something had to be done to Jesus.

*I'll bet that was a sight! Jesus of Nazareth — the disrupter — the trouble maker — the terrorist.*

Now some of his followers were proclaiming this man to be the Messiah — the Son of God. The situation was getting out of hand. Naturally the man was arrested.

"My God, my God, why have you forsaken me?" Jesus weakly cried out from the cross.

Dark clouds began quickly rolling in. The sky was turning black and accentuated with soundless erratic flashes of lightning.

*Must be a storm coming,* thought Longinus. He turned to the closest two Legionnaires and commanded, "Start a fire to give us some light to work with."

Longinus walked over to the foot of the cross. Some of his men were crouched down and casting dice to see who would get the Nazarene's robe.

*The man is still alive, and they are gambling for his bloody rags?*

*There was a time my soldiers would have feared acting such a way in front of me.*

*What has happened?*

*Why can't I elicit the same response anymore?*

*Where is their discipline?*

*I command this unit, yet the caliber of soldier I'm getting more and more seems almost mindless. Today they were mostly recruits from the western provinces — Hispana, Gallia, Germania, Raetia, Noricum, and Africa. They wanted to escape poverty so they joined the Legion in hopes of getting a bed and fed. Many took common-law wives during the campaigns, thus expanding Roman influence to the outskirts of the provinces and ensuring new generations of recruits for the sixty Legions. They learned military tactics well enough, and how to kill quickly and efficiently, but something was lacking — something was missing. Character. That was it. Oh they followed orders all right, but their character had not been honed. Their character had not been finely tuned.*

Two local thieves were also being crucified, one on either side of the Nazarene.

Longinus took a knee and looked up.

*Those thieves are actually guilty. They're young and strong. They'll last a while. But the carpenter ...*

"I thirst," croaked Jesus' voice weakly.

One of the Legionnaires took a sponge and soaked it in wine. He stuck it onto the end of a spear and hoisted it up to the Nazarene's lips.

The sky was almost completely black now with great streaks of lightning and booming cracks of thunder. It was as if the afternoon had turned to the darkest of nights.

Longinus picked up a pebble and tossed it to the side. He thought for a second.

*I can end this man's pain, this Jesus of Nazareth.*

He looked towards his left and saw the long spears which had been professionally racked by his soldiers.

Longinus stood up, walked over and selected the closest spear to him.

*Sadducees and Pharisees be damned.*

*I can end this man's misery now.*

One of the Legionnaires throwing dice saw what his Commander was doing and immediately jumped up.

"Here sir, let me do that."

Longinus hefted the spear in his hands.

"No, I'll do it," Longinus replied.

He walked to the foot of the cross, spear in hand. Looking up, he saw the battered body of Jesus, barely alive.

*The man is in agony. I'm going to finish this.*

Jesus looked skyward. "It is finished," he said weakly. "Father, into your hands I commend my spirit."

Then his head fell with chin to his chest, and his body went limp on the cross.

The mind of Longinus was determined. He stepped forward and raised the spear.

*It ends now,* he thought to himself.

Without emotion he thrust the spear upwards and into the right side chest of Jesus, just between the ribs.

Immediately Longinus felt a shock as if struck by lightning. For a second he thought he saw light emanating from the wound as tiny droplets of vermillion blood sprayed across his hands and face. Then sanguineous blood quickly poured down the blade and shaft of the spear. Longinus stumbled back dropping the spear and frantically began wiping the blood from his face. He suddenly felt intense remorse. He was ashamed of who he was and what he had just done. He felt guilt for his countrymen and scorn for his leaders. It flashed through his mind that he had just become a pawn for Hades.

Longinus sank to his knees and bowed his head. Several Legionnaires saw what was happening and rushed to their Commanders side. They tried to pick him up but as soon as they touched him they were tossed aback as if Mount Vesuvius had erupted.

Longinus rocked back and forth on his knees as tears streamed down his cheeks. He wrapped his arms around himself and sobbed inconsolably.

"Are you all right sir?" shouted one of the Legionnaires over the crackling of the thunder and the sudden downpour of rain.

Longinus pushed himself up and picked up the spear. He broke it in half across his knee and looked up. Torrents of rain and tears streaked down his face washing off the blood as he stared at the man called Jesus.

Dropping the pieces of spear, Longinus raised both arms skyward and said, "Surely this man was the Son of God."

# *PRESENT DAY*

*The first thing I'm going to tell my successor is to watch the generals, and to avoid feeling that just because they were military men their opinions on military matters were worth a damn.*

John F. Kennedy
1917 — 1963
President of the United States

# *CHAPTER ONE*

# *WHITE HOUSE BRIEFING*

Snow fell the night before, and a crisp shimmering blanket of it transformed the South Lawn and Lafayette Park into a frosty winter wonderland. Washington DC was beautiful this time of year for those who worked around the clock to safeguard freedom. For many, the seat of power for that freedom lies in the Executive Branch of the United States, otherwise known as the Office of the President. Since the year 1800 with the Presidency of John Adams, the official residence of every American President has been the White House.

Located at 1600 Pennsylvania Avenue NW in Washington DC — the White House complex includes the Executive Residence, the East Wing, the West Wing, the Eisenhower Executive Office Building, and a guest residence known as Blair House. The President's Executive Residence is composed of six stories, two of which are underground. The first floor of the West Wing includes the Oval Office from which the President conducts his most sensitive work.

The interior decor and seating arrangements can vary, but in the Oval Office today there are two large three-seat beige sofas facing each other and parallel to the President's Resolute Desk. This morning the Oval Office was hosting a flurry of Top Secret activity.

Top Secret?

Executive Order 13526 established the US classification information system. Top Secret is the highest level of classified information there is. To publicly reveal such information is said to cause grave harm to the national security. Even certain Top Secret information is further broken down into Sensitive Compartmented Information, or SCI. This type of information can be openly read inside a Sensitive Compartmented Information Facility, or SCIF. The Oval Office meets this strict criteria. It is not uncommon for classified information to be kept close-hold for various reasons — many of them political. Information is power, or so they say.

President Donald Trump had just returned to the White House from a campaign stop in San Antonio Texas. He was there to support the reelection efforts of his good friend Senator Ted Cruz. As usual, the President brought back with him his favorite pizza from Pizza Classics, and had a feast laid out on tables in the Oval Office for his advisors present. Spread out on the couches facing each other were four of President Donald Trump's most trusted colleagues: Chief of Staff of the Army General Braxton Matthews, Director of the National Security Agency (NSA) Teresa Cenni, Director of the Central Intelligence Agency (CIA) Anna Kliner, and Counselor to the President, Metta Ngernluan.

Metta Ngernluan's family legally immigrated to the United States from Laos when she was just two years old. Her father taught physics at Central Michigan University, and her mother was an accomplished concert pianist. Metta became a piano virtuoso by the age of five, and graduated magna cum laude from Harvard Law School at the age of twenty-three. She resigned as Team Chief of the Law Division of the Ford Motor Company when President Trump came calling. Metta never looked back.

"Okay Metta," said President Trump, "what's the scoop?"

The Counselor to the President cleared her throat.

"Sir," said Metta, "President Xi Jinping will be meeting with you for dinner this Friday at Mar-a-Lago. On the plate is the North Korean trade summit, the arming of Taiwan, ASEAN expansion, and Pacific Theater tariff requirements."

President Trump was leaning forward in his chair and was, as usual, listening intently with total focus.

"Xi is a real tough cookie. Go on," he said.

Metta reached for the manila folder on her lap with the red top secret coversheet and flipped it open. "Sir," she said, "as you know, the Xi Jinping regime is obsessed with esoteric knowledge and the occult."

"Mmm," mused President Trump, "uh-huh." He leaned back in his chair and looked at the stack of folders flowing out of his *In Box*. He extracted the top one and opened it.

"And this is about the new business then?"

"Yes sir," said Metta. "President Xi has ordered a worldwide search for ancient artifacts that have certain historical significance. He feels it will unify his people. In particular, he's searching for artifacts that have an association with mystical power. Recently his archeology teams have been observed in Rome, Istanbul, and Vienna. They are buying up every relic they can get their hands on pertaining to Judeo-Christian and Islamic beliefs."

"But why Judeo-Christian and Islam?" asked President Trump.

Metta said, "China as a communist country is officially atheist, however the Xi Jinping regime's plan is to house these items in their own museums creating displays of artifacts to ridicule and discredit the major religions of the world as fiction. Their hope is to demonstrate to their people that religion is, in the words of Karl Marx, the opium of the people. That being said sir, at this time I would like to turn it over to Director Cenni who will brief you on Operation TIMELESS DESTINY."

President Trump smiled. He was always amused by the cover phrases and codewords used to label secret operations.

"Go ahead," said the President.

NSA Director Teresa Cenni was a graduate of the University of Hawaii. A former surfer turned career US Navy Signal Corps officer, she still wore the Bulova surfboard chronograph watch with orange Swiss Tropic strap that her parents had given her for her twenty-fifth birthday. Teresa Cenni was named after her great grandmother — La Contessa Teresa di Cenni, whose claim to fame was that her husband, Santino, was the first to open a Bugatti dealership in Milan. She had made a name for herself in the satellite and imagery field, and had retired at the rank of Vice Admiral. Shortly thereafter she was appointed by President Trump as his personal choice for NSA Director.

Director Cenni stood up to address the President.

“Please sit and make yourself comfortable, Teresa,” said President Trump gesturing to the sofa.

“Sir,” said Teresa, “the following information has all been verified through our high surveillance platforms including RAMPART, PRISM, and MYSTIC, and also with DIA’s STONE GHOST.”

President Trump nodded his head approvingly.

“Sir, are you familiar with the Spear of Destiny story?”

President Trump leaned forward in his chair and said, “Spear of Destiny? Yeah, I seem to remember seeing something about that on the History Channel. It was the spear that pierced Christ’s side at the crucifixion, wasn’t it?”

“Yes sir,” replied Teresa. “It’s known by several names — the Spear of Destiny — the Holy Lance — the Longinus Spear. The first historical reference we have of it is at the crucifixion when it was carried away by Joseph of Arimathea. Then in 570 AD a nomad describes the spear resting with a crown of thorns in the Basilica on Mount Zion. The relic is supposedly seen in Jerusalem at the Church of the Holy Sepulcher by Saint Gregory in 585 AD. In 614 AD the Holy Lance was captured when Jerusalem was sacked by invading Persians and brought to Constantinople. It ended up being housed in the Saint Sophia Mosque in Istanbul. In 1244 the Holy Lance was sold to King Louis IX of France. After the French Revolution it was taken to Constantinople again where it was kept until 1492 when it was seized by Turk Sultan Bayezid II and sent to Pope Innocent VIII. The Holy Lance is next moved to Nuremberg Germany and housed until more battles with the French caused it to be moved once again, this time to Linz and finally Vienna in 1805 to the Hofburg Palace

Museum. In 1938 Hitler marched into Austria with his armies and seized the Holy Spear. Hitler had it buried beneath his Nuremberg fortress where it remained until he committed suicide in April 1945. Then it was recovered by Patton's Third Army and placed back into the Hofburg Palace Museum on 6 January 1946, where it has remained ever since. The Longinus Spear is currently part of the collection in the Imperial Treasure Room."

"Fascinating," replied President Trump. "Please continue."

Teresa explained, "It appears that the Chinese have reached an agreement with the Hofburg Palace to make an exact replica of the Longinus Spear, for a sizable monetary contribution to the museum of course. They will be sending a Chinese archeological team to Vienna to replicate the spear this week. Our concern is there could be an attempt to replace the original spear with the duplicate. Once the Chinese would have the spear they would never give it up."

Teresa studied the President's face as he was filtering everything she had just told him.

"I see," said President Trump. "And just why is the spear important to us?"

Teresa glanced at the others in the room and then back at President Trump.

"Well sir, it has long been believed that armies which march behind the Spear of Destiny are invincible."

President Trump studied Teresa's face for a second.

"Hmm. Then I guess it's important we make sure the original spear doesn't fall into President Xi's hands. Thank you Teresa. Director Kliner?"

"Yes sir," replied CIA Director Anna Kliner.

"So what's your take on all this?" asked the President.

Anna Kliner was a former military brat. She was the honor graduate in her Air Force ROTC class at Yale University, and received her commission as an Intelligence officer. She served for over thirty years and retired as a Lieutenant General, with her final assignment being as Director of the Defense Intelligence Agency (DIA) on Joint Base Anacostia-Bolling in Washington DC. President Trump had been impressed with her intelligence reports proving that the COVID-19 virus was actually specifically engineered and weaponized militarily as a bio-weapon, and that China had deliberately released it through its civilian airline travelers to crash world economies and, hopefully, crash President Trump's reelection bid. China hated Trump's tariffs, trade restrictions, and tough military posturing in the pacific. They wanted him gone. So it was no surprise to anyone that President Trump appointed Anna as his CIA Director.

"Sir, there could be a link between the Chinese archeological team going after the Longinus Spear and the disappearance of their Admiral Shui Gui last week in the Bahamas."

Anna waited for a response from the President.

President Trump picked up a pen from his desk and started writing inside the folder. After a few seconds he asked, "What kind of link?"

"Sir, do you remember when we briefed you on the World War Two device codenamed Die Glocke, the Bell?"

"Yes, I certainly do," replied President Trump. "The alleged Nazi time machine, right?"

"Yes sir," replied Anna, "and supposedly a myth, but if you

remember, during the course of our monitoring we intercepted phone messages of Chinese Admiral Shui Gui and a German national Fräulein Ulka Brunträger discussing Die Glocke, with the Chinese indicating a desire to purchase the technology."

"Okay," said the President.

Anna said, "Well sir, last week in Coopers Town on the Bahamian Island of Abaco there was an explosion at CHEC and a warehouse was destroyed …"

"What's CHEC?" asked President Trump.

"The Chinese Harbor Engineering Company, sir," answered Anna. "We suspect that the Die Glocke mechanism was in the warehouse, but we were never able to verify it because the port is controlled by the Chinese Navy."

"I see," said the President.

"Also," Anna continued, "we were never able to verify what happened to Admiral Shui Gui. He hasn't been heard from since. He seems to have just disappeared from view."

President Trump asked, "So, he could have been killed in the explosion, along with the destruction of the Bell, but we just don't know? Is that right?"

"I'm afraid so sir," sighed Anna.

"Anything else Anna?" asked the President.

"No sir, that's it."

"Okay," said President Trump. "Braxton, what do you have?"

President Trump looked over at General Matthews.

Four-star General Braxton Matthews graduated at the top of his class from West Point. He was a career Special Forces officer, with multiple worldwide command and staff tours. Matthews had impressed President Trump so much by his initiatives to eradicate the ISIS caliphate that Trump made him his Army Chief of Staff. His experience with intelligence organizations was that they were interconnected by a surprisingly delicate structure, and loathed interfacing with each other to share information. US intelligence had become an intricate web where one hand didn't know what the other hand was doing. Information was provided too late or not at all. He swore to himself that if ever given the chance he would provide accurate information and as timely as possible.

Matthews said, "Sir, we believe our man in Zurich destroyed the Abaco warehouse. And the only possible reason for him to destroy it would be that Die Glocke was in it."

Trump resumed writing in the folder.

"And since Admiral Shui Gui has disappeared, I think our guy took care of him as well," said Matthews.

Donald Trump stopped writing and looked at General Matthews.

"Took care of?" asked President Trump. "You mean killed?"

"Yes sir," answered Matthews.

"What was that guy's name again?" asked the President.

"Ross, sir," answered Matthews, "Captain James Ross."

President Trump asked, "Have you been in contact with Ross?"

Matthews frowned. "Ah, sir, that's the problem. No one has."

"What do you mean?" asked the President.

Matthews said, "We've attempted to contact him, but to no avail. Our assets in the field can't find him. No one seems to know where he is. Ross seems to have disappeared as well."

"Disappeared?" asked the President.

"Yes sir. For now anyway. But I personally know Captain Ross, sir. We've worked together many times in the past. If he has the means, he'll contact us."

"Is it possible that Captain Ross died as a result of the explosion?" asked the President.

Matthews shook his head.

"We don't think so, sir. His plane was seen crashing into the Chinese warehouse, but AWACS surveillance picked up heat signatures of two people leaving the aircraft, possibly in a gyroplane. We lost track of them over the Triangle."

President Trump looked perplexed.

"What Triangle?" asked the President.

Matthews clasped his hands together on his lap. "Ah — the Bermuda Triangle, sir."

Trump steeled his gaze and let out a low whistle. He threw the top secret folder on top of the Resolute desk and leaned back in his chair.

"Look," said the President, "does this Die Glocke, or Bell, or whatever the hell it is actually work? Does it really function? I mean, does the damn thing even exist?"

NSA Director Cenni tried to reassure the President.

"Sir, we have no solid intelligence that it does."

Metta Ngernluan looked at her colleagues for any other comments. The room was silent.

President Donald Trump studied the four faces of his most trusted staff officers sitting in from of him.

"Ladies and gentlemen, it appears to me we have lots of work to do. I want you to monitor this situation very closely. Brief me daily. I'm very concerned about the Chinese attempt to obtain the Spear of Destiny. That feat could give China a very needed military albeit psychological advantage. And I want to know everything that is going on with this time-travel device, if in fact said device actually exists."

All four staff members simultaneously glanced at each other and nodded affirmatively.

"Keep me informed. Okay, that's it for now," said President Trump.

The four staff officers rose to attention.

"And Braxton …"

"Sir?" said Matthews.

Trump stood up and said with conviction, "Find Captain Ross."

# *CHAPTER TWO*

# *VISIONS*

It was just after midnight. A time referred to as *the witching hour.*

Lin Sparrow tossed and turned in the bed. Sweat was beading on her forehead. A low guttural moan emanated from her throat and pushed through her pursed lips. Lin was asleep and dreaming. It was the same identical dream she'd had for the past three nights. The dream always started the same way …

It was the most colorful season of the year — autumn — and the weather was turning crisp and cold.

Orangish-brown leaves covered the ground, and the crunch of them under your feet was comforting.

It was twilight — that time when the sun has just set, and the earth is neither completely lit nor completely dark.

The date was October 31.

Halloween.

Lin remembered when her fiancé, Captain James Ross, had proposed marriage to her, and how those plans had been brutally eviscerated by the international terrorist financier, Wolfram von Lugoff, otherwise known as the Professor. James Ross had somehow been able to travel back in time and save her, with the help of a machine — a World War II Nazi time machine.

*Fantastic.*

But now Lin and Ross had finished their time-travel trip back to the present.

They both stepped out of the machine.

They were home.

Home again.

Time to fall in love.

Time to live their life.

Together.

Together — forever.

And there in front of her was the Roman Colosseum.

*It's what I always dreamed of.*

And the Arch of Constantine.

*I'm so happy.*

And the …

*Wait a minute.*

*Something's wrong!*

Large colorful flags representing all countries were flapping everywhere in the brisk autumn wind.

*Perhaps it was a fair?*

*Maybe it was some joyous celebration?*

Huge blood-red banners hung from the sides of buildings, proclaiming the People's Republic of China.

*China?*

And then she saw it and gasped.

Roman soldiers, from Legions long ago lost, now seemed to be marching all around. Their uniforms were ancient, but their shields where emblazoned blood-red with a large gold star with four small gold stars offset in an arc.

*No!*

Roman Legionnaires, armed with lances, were dragging people, and beating people, and laughing. All this against a backdrop of broken crucified bodies hanging from thousands of wooden crosses.

*Something is wrong!*

*This can't be!*

Then modern Chinese soldiers started marching alongside the Roman soldiers. They were allies. The Chinese soldiers appeared to be supervising.

*Chinese and Roman soldiers?*

Lin now began to shiver in her bed as the dream continued.

Suddenly the sky lit up with a huge blue-green video screen.

Splashing across it in blood-red lettering were messages.

"Socialism makes you Free."

"All Power to the State."

"The State is your Religion."

"Your Leader Loves You."

*Your Leader Loves You?*

*What in the world is this?*

*What has happened?*

*This is a nightmare!*

Then more messages flashed across the screen …

"Federal Holiday."

"Celebration All Week."

And then finally …

"Beloved Founding Father — Xi Jinping."

The video screen showed Xi as a very old man.

*This can't be!*

The picture on the screen then changed to the red Chinese flag with an ancient Roman spear now piercing the middle of the large gold star.

*NO!*

*It can't be!*

*What is this?*

*What has happened?*

*Something's wrong!*

*Something is terribly, horribly wrong!*

Ross and Lin stood hand-in-hand staring at this macabre nightmare when suddenly a Chinese soldier magically appeared in front of them.

"Halt!" the woman screamed.

The pair looked incredulously as the Chinese soldier leveled an ancient Roman lance at them.

"Traitors!" yelled the female Chinese soldier.

Ross gripped Lin's hand all the tighter.

"Go to hell," spat Ross back defiantly.

The Chinese soldier thrust the lance forward and tore through Ross's chest as he turned to Lin trying to shield her with his body.

"… love you … Lin …" Ross gasped, smiling reassuringly.

"… always …"

Then he collapsed into her arms.

*Noooooooooooo!*

Lin Sparrow awoke at five o'clock in the morning with the jolt of an electric spark.

Her nude body was glistening from head to toe with trickles of cold salty sweat.

She looked over at James Ross.

*Still asleep.*

So as not to awaken him, she delicately peeled off the thin white bedsheet that had been covering her, and tiptoed carefully into the small bathroom. For the past three days they both had been staying in one of the spare bedroom living quarters on the second floor of Emanuel's place in Zurich Switzerland. Emanuel was the enigmatic Philippine taxicab driver who had shared many of their past adventures.

Founded by the Romans just over two thousand years ago, Zurich has a population of almost two million, making it the largest city in Switzerland. It is one of the world's busiest economic financial centers as it has its own stock exchange. Its low tax rate draws many overseas corporations to position their headquarters there. The city is a plethora of culture, boasting festivals, art galleries, museums, symphonies, theater, opera, ballet, and multiple sporting events. Zurich is also the richest metropolitan area in Europe, and the world's largest gold bullion trading center. It's the home of many 5-star luxury hotels and restaurants, one in particular being the Asiatisches Essen Philippine Restaurant.

German for "Asian Food," *Asiatisches Essen* was owned by Emanuel's cousin Lailani and her husband Lars. Emanuel had lived in a room on the second floor, and after consulting with his cousin, allowed Ross and Lin to board in one of the other spare upstairs bedrooms. But Emanuel was gone now, having mysteriously vanished last week while piloting the Horten 229 V9 over the Bahamian Island of Abaco.

Lin clicked on the lights and examined her face in the large mirror hanging above the ancient porcelain sink.

*This is crazy.*

*I've had the same dream, over and over now, for three nights.*

*Something is up.*

*Something is going to happen to us.*

*I can see it.*

*I can feel it.*

*I know it.*

*My mother said I was a seer.*

*My father said I had the gift.*

*I've always had it.*

*Back home, our neighbors called it witchcraft.*

*Others called it clairvoyance.*

*Whatever its name — I've got it.*

She knew these dreams were more than nightmares or visions.

They were memories.

Lin stared deeply into the brown eyes analyzing her in the mirror.

She picked up the tube of minty Crest toothpaste and squeezed a dab out onto her pink toothbrush. Brushing her teeth quickly, Lin then gargled with an AAFES antiseptic mouthwash, courtesy the local Base Exchange, and spat the residue out into the sink.

Lin walked over to the shower stall and slid open the transparent glass door, stepped inside, and then closed the door behind her.

With hot water jets pulsating, Lin scrubbed herself in the steamy shower with wild cherry blossom Suave deep moisturizing bodywash and lathered her hair with strawberry TRESemmé moisturizing shampoo. She thoroughly rinsed herself off with tepid water, and then stepped out of the shower. Grabbing a large red terrycloth towel, she dried herself off.

Back in the bedroom, Lin put on a sheer pair of panties and matching bra. Then she selected an ivy gold knee-length silk skirt and a Wimbledon white blouse. She slipped a two-baht gold chain with matching Buddha around her neck, and strapped a stainless steel Citizen Eco-drive ProMaster Diver watch with black rubber strap onto her left wrist. She splashed Obsession eau de parfum on her neck, and rubbed her wrists together with a dash.

Lin sat down on the bed and looked at herself in the bedroom mirror.

She was five-feet-nine-inches tall.

That was tall for a Malaysian lady.

But Lin was only half Malay.

She was a mixture of East and West, just like her American boyfriend Captain James Ross.

Lin's mother, Mira Wan Tengku, was Malay, and her father, Lieutenant Alastair Jasper Sparrow, had been a British Special Air Service officer assigned to their embassy in Kuala Lumpur. He was killed from a terrorist bomb explosion when Lin was just a child. She had never really gotten to know her father all that well. Her mother never remarried, and had kept the last name of Sparrow.

Lin was twenty-six years old now.

She continued staring at herself in the mirror.

Her silky raven locks cascaded slightly below her shoulders, with bangs that stopped just above her eyebrows. She had long sexy eyelashes, and a petite nose that was slightly upturned. Her eyes were deep brown almonds that sparkled in the light, and her mouth was large and captivatingly beautiful, with glistening full lips. Her skin was very smooth with almost no body hair. As with most Asian women, her legs were naturally satiny smooth and never required shaving. She kept her fingernails cut short and unpainted, however she did apply a clear polish to her toenails. Her calves were muscled, her stomach flat, and at times she exhibited unusual strength.

Lin reached over to the nightstand and picked up a cosmetic brush to apply a small trace of rouge blush powder to her half Western cheeks.

When she was done, she looked around and slipped her feet into well worn ebony three-inch-heeled pumps.

Lin used to serve as Executive Personal Secretary to the Honorable Simon Watlington, the United States Ambassador to Malaysia. That was also when she first met James Ross. That civil service job had been rewarding, but at a cost to her dignity and self-respect. It just became too unbearable for her to work at the US Embassy in Kuala Lumpur. She simply could not stand to work, day after day, within the labyrinth of backstabbing political machinations. Lin had always wanted a job that she could be proud of. She wanted to do something that would make a difference in peoples' lives. She wanted to have a sense of actually helping people, of making the world a little better place to live in. She wanted to give something of herself back to the people of Malaysia. Consequently, she enrolled in an accelerated evening studies program at the Puteri Nursing College, and completed her Bachelor of Science in Nursing degree. She served for a time as a critical care registered nurse in the emergency room of the Twin Towers Medical Center for Doctor Arjinderpal Sekhon in Kuala Lumpur, Malaysia. But then she started to have more dreams and visions — dreams and visions which included her then-boyfriend, James Ross, and which led to more and more adventures. Adventures which carried her across the globe and literally into and out of the jaws of death. And then Ross had proposed marriage, and she had accepted.

Lin heard a rustle of sheets behind her and glanced in the mirror to see Ross getting up.

"Good morning my beautiful lovely darling," said James Ross, stretching his arms and yawning.

Lin turned and wrapped her arms around Ross's neck and kissed him passionately. He responded and placed his hands on her waist.

"Good morning my love," purred Lin.

Lin looked into the deep pools of James Ross's piercing dark brown eyes.

*Am I really engaged to this man?*

She looked at the shards of hair hanging across his forehead that would never stay in place.

*Is this for real?*

*Am I really here?*

She looked at the lips that had always spoken the truth to her and satisfied herself that *yes,* this was indeed real and happening.

She had to be sure, since just last week she had been in Kecksburg Pennsylvania in 1965, having been transported there by Ross in Die Glocke — the Bell — the Nazi time machine. But they had found another Die Glocke in Kecksburg, along with an attempt to resurrect the Third Reich, and Ross destroyed all of it. And now here they were back in Zurich.

*Why did I love this man?* pondered Lin.

*James has always been troubled by the despair he sees in the world.*

*He has always been troubled when he sees good people suffer.*

*He has always been troubled when he sees evil doers triumph.*

*James sought out the answers from his faith.*

*His is the Christian faith.*

*His is the belief in the Christian God.*

*He questions why God would allow atrocities to occur rampant and flourish throughout the world.*

*Why does God allow innocents to be savagely raped and butchered?*

*Why does God allow children to be abused by the very institutions sworn to protect them and give them hope?*

*Why does God allow the existence of murder and war, disease and famine, injustice and evil?*

*Why does God allow his greatest creation — human beings — to die?*

*James' faith is a great mystery to him.*

*His faith promises salvation if you just believe.*

*But what James Ross came to understand, is that belief is not enough.*

*He realized that a human being has to act.*

*He realized that a human being has to create justice, seek truth, practice compassion, and gain wisdom.*

*Most importantly, James realized that a human being has to act with love.*

*He realized there were three questions to answer in life:*

*What is worth dying for?*

*What is worth living for?*

*What is most precious in the world?*

*To James Ross, the answer he found was always the same.*

*The answer —*

*— is love.*

Lin was now engaged to James Ross.

*Captain and Mrs. James Ross,* she mused.

*He was still on thirty days of leave from the US Army.*

*We should be planning our wedding.*

*We should be looking forward to a life together.*

*Together.*

*Forever.*

Lin thought for a second …

She knew Ross was twenty-nine years old.

*He's really tall too, probably six-foot-three I would guess, and around a hundred and eighty-five pounds or so.*

*With lovely piercing dark brown eyes, and sexy shards of brown hair hanging across his forehead that would never stay in place.*

*He was half Thai, half caucasian.*

*He was a Captain in the United States Army Special Forces.*

*He saved my life.*

*And I love him.*

*Oh I love him so.*

Ross squinted at the luminescent dial of his Benrus Type I divers watch.

It was 0603 hours.

He rolled out of bed and staggered nude into the bathroom, flicking on the lights and fan.

He didn't really need anyone to wake him up.

As usual, he had mentally egressed himself to wake up through the sheer force of his will.

Ever since he had attended the Special Forces Qualification Course at Fort Bragg, he could just somehow *will* his body to wake up at anytime. It wasn't magical. It was just something that many SF soldiers were capable of doing.

Ross walked over and slid open the transparent glass doors of the shower stall and stepped in, closing them behind him.

Pulling the plastic power jet handles outward, he straightened his arms and leaned forward, pressing both of his palms against the shower wall under the needling spray. Slowly, he lowered his head and allowed the heavy stream of hot pulsating water to cascade over his lean muscular body.

Ross completed the shower in his usual four minutes. He stepped out of the shower stall and wrapped one of the huge red terrycloth towels around his waist.

Wiping his right hand across the steam covered mirror, he looked at himself.

He fingered his mornings worth of stubble and reached for his AAFES shave gel. With a liberal amount of Army-Air-Force-Exchange-Services shave gel on, he slowly glided his razor across his face. He lowered his head towards the sink and splashed hot water across his face to rinse off the remaining residue. As if on cue, he poured Aqua Velva aftershave into his cupped left hand and slapped it on his face. Now he was awake.

Ross sauntered to the closet, opened his suitcase, and pulled out his clothes. His traveling ensemble was pretty much the same always. He stepped into a pair of yellow plaid boxer shorts. Then he put on a white cotton shirt with tiny burgundy pinstripes running vertically. He cinched the collar with a narrow black necktie with a four-in-hand knot. Then he pulled on a black pair of pants with a black leather belt, black stretch socks, and stepped into his black leather shoes. And he topped it all off with his black suit coat.

Ross took a quick glance at himself in the bedroom mirror. He ran a comb through the thick shards of dark brown hair hanging across his forehead that would never stay in place. They just fell right back down again.

*The hell with it,* smiled Ross.

Ross came over and sat next to Lin on the bed. He delicately reached out, taking both her hands in his, and kissed them. He held her hands gently while he spoke.

"Lin, I've still got eight days left on my leave," said Ross. "We need to get married now."

Lin nervously fingered the engagement ring Ross had given her. It was a one carat diamond, set in a four prong eighteen karat gold ring. She listened with rapt attention.

"We could get married in the US Consular Office downtown. It's on Dufourstarsse. Would that be okay with you, Lin?"

"Yes," gushed Lin, "yes that's great. Let's do it right away."

"And then we'll be able to get your military identification dependent card, and I'll be able to go on the DEERS website and enroll you."

"What's DEERS again?" asked Lin puzzling.

"DEERS is the Defense Enrollment Eligibility Reporting System. That's where I enroll you for healthcare, dental care, and all the rest as my dependent."

"Okay," said Lin. "Let's do it soon. But first Darling, I have something very important to tell you."

Ross already guessed.

"The dreams, isn't it? It's the dreams."

"Yes," said Lin. "They are simply horrific."

Ross knew better than to question Lin Sparrow's dreams. They had always turned out to be metaphors for the truth. They were in fact visions of a possible future. A future, that if not changed, if not acted upon, would materialize as the present. And the visions had always saved his life by bringing Lin to him.

"What was the latest one, the one this morning?"

Lin stood up and started pacing about.

"It began with both of us in Rome. Then, I started to see ancient Roman Legionnaire soldiers and present day Chinese soldiers working together. Working together — to enslave people. The world was topsy-turvy."

"Oh boy," said Ross. "And what?"

Lin looked at Ross with desperate eyes.

"And we were both in trouble from a Chinese soldier."

"I see," said Ross.

Ross thought for a second.

"I'll tell you what Lin, let's put the visions on hold for a while and let me call Emanuel's cousin Lailani. Maybe we can grab some breakfast. What do you say?"

"Okay. Let's have breakfast," said Lin.

Ross picked up the Samsung Galaxy Stratosphere II that he had purchased from a local vendor in Berlin at the Tempelhof Park. He opened up his contacts and scrolled through until he found Lailani's number. Then he pressed the *call* button.

*Bzzz.*

*Bzzz.*

*Bzzz.*

Picking up her phone, Lailani pressed the little green *accept call* button and responded.

"Hello?"

"Good morning Lailani. I'm sorry to disturb you so early."

"No, no James. We've been up for a while. Are you and Lin ready for some breakfast?"

"We sure are," replied Ross.

"Come on down then. See you in a bit. Oh and James …" said Lailani.

"Yeah?"

"What is that thing in our garage?"

# *CHAPTER THREE*

# *BUREAU #18*

Near Tiananmen Square at number 100 Xiyuan Haidian District in Beijing China is located quite an interesting complex of buildings. It could be the manufacturing hub for a Chinese automobile corporation, or perhaps the headquarters of an information technology conglomerate. But it is neither of these. The buildings appear relatively mundane except for the high walls, fences, barbed wire, armed guards, and rooftops festooned with antennas. Named the Yidongyuan Compound, it houses the headquarters for the Chinese Ministry of State Security (MSS). The MSS is the principal intelligence, national security, and secret police agency in the communist People's Republic of China. The MSS is one of the world's largest and most secretive intelligence organizations, and has multiple branch offices located throughout China. Their manpower is over 110,000 strong. The motto of the MSS is: "To serve the people firmly and purely, to reassure the Party, to contribute, to be able to fight hard, and to win."

There are thousands of Chinese spies located in the United States actively engaging in espionage from the board room to the dorm room. For several years American Democrat Party policies allowed thousands of Chinese operatives to enter the United States through its wide open southern border. Trained military age operators crossed over illegally unchecked. In 2013 it was even revealed that California Democrat US Senator Dianne Feinstein had unknowingly employed, for over 20 years, a chauffeur who was an agent of the Chinese Ministry of State Security.

The MSS consists of 18 separate bureaus broken down into information technology, counterintelligence, human intelligence, cyber warfare, official and non-official cover operations, trade secret acquisitions, intellectual property theft, foreign university influencing, research institute espionage, foreign governmental agency infiltration, and assassinations. Of these, Bureau #18 is located on the 7th floor of building 1206. Today in room 23 of Bureau #18 there is a very special meeting taking place. Room 23 is a SCIF. All Top Secret material discussed inside would never leave the room. If something ever went wrong with an operation, the planner would be killed before President Xi Jinping would be embarrassed. Bureau #18 conducts and manages all clandestine intelligence operations in and against the United States. Bureau #18 also handles assassinations. This morning, six top executive officers of the MSS sat around a long mahogany table in room 23. They were discussing a two tiered plan of attack.

“Rear Admiral Shui Gui’s death must be avenged,” seethed General Yanjin Yixin. “The President demands retaliation, and retaliate we will. How soon will the team be ready?”

“Sir,” replied Colonel Bai Weng, “it’s all set for this weekend.”

“Explain,” said the General.

“Sir, we have already sent the team to Vienna Austria. Their official cover is as a People’s Archeology Research Team. Their official mission is to construct an exact replica of the Spear of Destiny for inclusion in the exhibit at the National Museum in Beijing.”

“And …” prodded the General.

Colonel Bai Weng said, “Their classified mission has two parts. Part one is to liberate the Spear of Destiny and replace the original with our own replica. Part two is to find the killer of Admiral Shui Gui and retaliate in kind.”

“Excellent. The Spear will be a sweet coup. The President is very excited about obtaining it and safeguarding it in his private residence. He feels possessing the Spear will only strengthen our country.”

Sycophantic smiles beamed across the faces at the table.

“Yes sir,” replied Colonel Weng.

“What about the team leader? Is he reliable?” asked General Yixin.

Colonel Bai Weng replied, “Sir, the team leader is a woman. She’s a highly skilled intelligence officer. Her name is Nü Jiangshi. She’s well-traveled, speaks fluent German and English, and has conducted assassinations before. She is known for being totally ruthless, disciplined, and her devotion to the State is beyond question.”

"Very good," said General Yixin. "Now, who is this man we are after? Who is the man responsible for Admiral Shui Gui's death?"

"The man our advanced team has identified is an American officer. Captain, US Army. His name is Ross. James Ross. He is one of their Special Forces assassins. A Green Beret. But there is one thing very curious."

"What's that?"

"We received reports that Captain Ross may be under charges from his superiors."

"Charges? For what?"

"Ah," said Colonel Weng sheepishly, "supposedly for illegally entering Switzerland with a diplomatic passport while on leave."

A cynical frown broke out across General Yixin's face as he sat back in his chair.

"Not a chance," he said. "This is not the prior administration. Those years are over. We lost our greatest political pawn. Back then, we had the President and his family in our pockets. Our million dollar payouts for their influence peddling schemes led directly to our country's power ascension over the world. Of course we also had to release and then control the bio-weapon known as COVID, but that was a relatively simple affair."

Heads around the table were nodding affirmatively.

"Destruction of the traditional American family was necessary. So we started subtly influencing their children in public schools and universities with our indoctrinated teachers. We taught them to hate and disrespect parental authority. Then we moved forward with destroying their traditional culture. The American Democrat Political

Party came in handy for that purpose. Our psychological operations experts were correct in surmising how easy it would be to manipulate their Democrat Party to submit to our will. They are composed of individuals who are totally corrupt after all. Money attracts them like gypsy moths to a light. And once we had the Democrat Party duped, it was easy to then introduce the racism tactic. We turned to their long-gone-centuries-old Civil War, and manipulated them to tear down hero statues, rename military bases, and basically alienate half of their own country. We managed to get a police defund movement up and running in all Democrat-led states, and even get their legal system to release violent criminals. The open border policy allowed us to infiltrate eighteen-thousand of our own operators into the United States for future missions, not to mention the other sixteen-million immigrants who entered illegally and are bankrupting their entire infrastructure. Perhaps our greatest coup was being able to tacitly manipulate their own military leaders through their corrupt politicians. This was extremely paramount to our mission success. We relied on their inherent narcissism. Remember when we brokered the deal to introduce Diversity-Equity-Inclusion training into the American military? We even coerced them to initiate Critical Race Theory at West Point. DEI and CRT are pure Marxist ideology. It wasn't long before we had their own Chairman of the Joint Chiefs telling Congress that he wanted to learn what 'white rage' was."

A cynical smile crept across General Yixin's face.

"We even had him apologizing to their entire military for walking to a Christian church with their President holding a bible. When we could destroy their history, culture, traditions, family, and religion, we knew we would win. Remember when we financially supported youthful radicals to organize race riots on their own streets? We were even able to influence some to deface their sacred Alamo shrine in Texas. How surprised the Americans seemed when the leaders of those organizations turned out to be mere money-hungry charlatans. Our 'Woke' program was pure communist theory straight out of the Marxist-Leninist Handbook. The intent was to divide the United States through manipulating social and mainstream media with deliberate lies. Divide and conquer — a tactic as old as time. It was utter nonsense infused into America by us. We manipulated half their country to hate the other half. We sought to create division and put into power those politicians who were monetarily beholden to us. The United States was ripe for a complete communist takeover. Unfortunately, most of our endeavors were dissolved by President Donald Trump once he was elected."

General Yixin looked around the table at his comrades.

"I find it hard to believe that the United States Army would discipline a Green Beret officer — one of their very best — because of misusing a passport," he chuckled.

The other five officers around the table looked at each other and automatically nodded their heads approvingly.

"Yes sir," said Lieutenant Colonel Bohai Xu. "There is no way the Americans would be that stupid today."

General Yixin pounded the table with his fist, startling the other officers.

“Just be sure we get the original Longinus Spear,” said Yixin. “President Xi Jinping is counting on it. And, make sure this American, this Captain Ross, dies a most horrible death. Dismissed”

“Yes sir!” said the other five officers in unison as they immediately stood to attention and saluted.

# *CHAPTER FOUR*

# *DIE GLOCKE*

Ross put on a red wool jacket and walked outside to the garage. His fingers momentarily clung to the frozen hasp securing the two large yellow painted barn-type doors as he flung them open. Gusts of late December snow blustered inside and swirled around the garage for a few seconds as Ross flipped on the bank of overhead florescent lights. There in the middle of the garage, flanked on one side by Emanuel's black 1972 Mercedes-Benz S-Class and on the other side by a green 2002 Citroën Xantia, sat the machine known as Die Glocke.

Back in 1944 when the Third Reich was falling apart, SS-Obersturmbannführer Otto Skorzeny had entrusted his friend, Obersturmführer Wilhelm von Lugoff, to safeguard Die Glocke. Die Glocke was actually designed to open a portal through time itself. It was a type of transporter to the past or the future. Through testing, Die Glocke was found to be able to transfer a man into the fourth dimension.

It *was* a time machine.

The Nazis planned enormous military applications for Die Glocke. The idea was to transport select troops into the time vortex to conduct military operations that would guarantee total victory and win the war for the Fatherland.

General Hans Kammler had been the engineer in charge of the V-2 missiles, and had been personally chosen by Himmler to lead the Die Glocke project. It's even believed that his complete disappearance at the end of the war had something to do with the machine. Some said he transported himself to the future, and then returned the Bell back to the past. General Kammler was one of the esteemed Councilors of the Interior. As an Obergruppenführer, Hans Kammler served the Third Reich with distinction. He had joined the Schutzstaffel — SS — and managed all SS engineer requirements, and was in charge of the Special Projects Division for the Führer. Special Projects Division included the Führer's wonder-weapons. These *wunderwaffe* were Hitler's gift to the future. Kammler oversaw everything, from the revolutionary Horten 229 jet flying wing aircraft to the breathtaking V-2 missile attack systems.

Operation CHRONOS was the codename for Nazi Germany's secret attempt to master space-time vortex compression. The Greek word for *time* is *chronos.* Chronos was considered a God in pre-Socratic Greek philosophy, and was the son of Uranus — God of the sky. Chronos wounded his father, or so the myth tells us, and from the blood was born the Furies — female spirits of vengeance and justice. The Nazis were obsessed with Teutonic and Norse myths. In Norse mythology, the world was depicted as a tree — the tree of the world —

known as Yggdrasil. Odin's Kingdom of the Nine Realms was attached to Yggdrasil. Chronos has been depicted as a serpent wrapped around Yggdrasil. The world will come to an end when the serpent releases its grip on Yggdrasil, or so it was believed in ancient times.

The Third Reich was using German Professor Albert Einstein's special and general relativity laws of physics for gravity as a curvature of space-time, and the relationship of time to gravity absence. The experiments utilized thorium-nitrate emulsion, beryllium-peroxide fusion, xerum-methane separation, and mercury displacement. They had produced the desired magnetic field separation outcomes at high intensity counter-rotating speeds. Nazi physicists and mechanical engineers had solved the issue of antigravity time dilation. The Henge test site was used for the antigravity propulsion trials. Soon the Germans had a working prototype.

The resulting manufactured device was about the size and weight of a sedan, only more so resembling a very large bell. Hence, its German codename became Die Glocke, or in English simply — the Bell. All this had been accomplished at the Riese facility near the Czechoslovakian border.

CHRONOS could be proved theoretically on the chalk board, but had the capacity to enter the realm of something mystical — something magical. It was as if science and magic had blended together.

The device was approximately nine or ten feet wide, and fifteen feet tall. It was made out of some type of metal that Ross could not identify. It looked heavy, probably four to five thousand pounds. Its color was a faded dark metallic gray. Electronic cables crisscrossed around its base and up to its top. There was a hatch with a nautical locking wheel on the front of the device. Circling around the top of the machine appeared to be small windows or reflecting mirrors. It was reminiscent of Wernher von Braun's early design for the NASA Mercury space capsule.

Ross thought, *Die Glocke is fantastic.*

*Time doesn't matter anymore.*

*Whoever possesses Die Glocke can master time.*

*The past and present can be brought together.*

*I should just destroy this damn machine right now.*

Then it appeared as if the snow stopped falling, just for an instant, and there was a stillness in the wind which caught his attention.

Lin Sparrow walked into the garage and motioned to Ross with her hand.

"Come on. Time for breakfast."

Ross walked over to Lin and took her hand. They both stared back at Die Glocke.

"It's really fantastic, isn't it?" said Lin.

"Yeah," replied Ross.

"I mean, to think a person can travel forwards and backwards in time, is just incredible," said Lin. "For instance, doctors could travel back and inoculate children for polio. Think of the thousands of lives that could be saved, millions actually."

Ross thought for a second.

"Very true," he said. "I guess my military background prejudices me to only think of the problems it could cause. I mean, what if someone took a nuclear weapon back and gave it to the Nazis, or Imperial Japan, or even Genghis Khan for that matter."

"Yes," said Lin. "Everything that glitters is not always gold."

# *CHAPTER FIVE*

# *CENTURIAN*

Built in the 13th century and located in the center of Vienna is the former imperial palace of the Habsburg Dynasty, known as the Hofburg. Today, the Hofburg Palace is the official workplace and residence of Austrian President Alexander Van der Bellen. Part of its 59 acreage houses the museum, with 21 rooms filled with rare antiquities dating back thousands of years. Some of these include imperial treasures of the Holy Roman Empire, ecclesiastical artifacts of emperors, and jewel encrusted crowns of former kings and queens. The Longinus Spear is also located there on public display.

"Closing time sir," said the museum guide.

Ludmila Durville looked at her watch. It was a 1968 Rolex Air King that her grandfather had given her before he passed away. The blade-type hands of her Rolex told her it was 1730 hours.

"What's that?" responded the man.

"Closing time sir," repeated Ludmila, this time tapping the crystal face of her Rolex. Ludmila was a 24-year-old Austrian-born brunette with a hint of Alsace-Lorraine in her high cheekbones. She graduated two years ago from the University of Vienna with a bachelors degree in Historical and Cultural Studies. From about the age of sixteen Ludmila had fallen in love with what could only be described as the Steampunk style. She wore modern versions of late nineteenth century period dresses to include matching shoes, stockings, even bras and panties. Today her five-foot-six-inch toned body was draped in a purple Steampunk corset dress, trimmed with white lace shoulders and dark brown leather bustier. Her feet were nestled in three-inch-heeled tan Victorian Spat Boots that buttoned up the side to her calves.

"Pardon me?" said the man.

Ludmila shifted her weight to her right foot and coquettishly placed her hands on her hips.

*He's handsome,* she thought. *Must be about thirty-five years old. Six feet tall at least. Shiny black hair. Suntanned. Looks fit. Maybe Italian,* she thought. *Dressed nice too. Black suit. Black overcoat. Classic good looks. Kinda sexy really. Reminds me of a young Sylvester Stallone. But there's something about his face. He's got sad eyes.*

This endeared her even more to him.

"I'm sorry but it's closing time sir," she repeated.

The man had been staring into a display case housing religious artifacts — the bible of Charlemagne the Great — the bejeweled crucifix of Napoleon Bonaparte — and the Longinus Spear. The Longinus Spear, also known as the Spear of Destiny and the Holy

Lance, was said to have mystical powers. It was said to be able to heal the sick, bring victory in battles, and even foretell the future.

"Pardon me. I guess time sort of slipped away. I'll be on my way now. Thank you," said the man.

*Poor guy,* thought Ludmila to herself.

The man turned and sauntered towards the exit of the museum. He strode through the revolving doors and was immediately hit with the windchill of a Viennese December. He pulled up his collar to the cold and briskly walked down the concrete steps to the parking lot. He pulled out his key fob and pressed the button to automatically open the doors of his black Audi A5 Cabriolet. Sitting inside he pressed the starter and the four-cylinder turbo engine purred to life.

*The spear looks the same,* he thought. *Some ornamentation has been added over the years, but it looks basically the same.*

He aggressively shifted gears as he drove through the Burgtor gate and onto Ringstrasse.

*Why did it have to be me?* he asked himself for the millionth time.

*Why did I have to pick up that spear?*

*Why?*

He shook his head.

*Jesus was already dead.*

*I thought I was giving him peace.*

Then the regret came once again.

*Why didn't I stop it?*

*Why didn't I speak up?*

Longinus did a racing gear change and pulled ahead of a Mercedes-Benz sedan.

*Why couldn't I have let it all alone?*

Longinus took a moment to remember. He had buried his wife and daughters centuries ago. He had watched everyone he ever loved pass away. Through the two millennia he had already lived since that tragic day, Longinus had come to realize that he was kept alive to protect the Spear of Destiny. His task was to safeguard the spear until the return of Jesus Christ.

*If only I could have left it alone.*

Longinus drove for ten minutes and then expertly parked his Audi A5 Cabriolet on Mariahilfer Strasse. He locked the Audi and crossed the street to his apartment. Once inside, Longinus changed into a magenta terrycloth robe and opened a bottle of wine. He poured himself a magnum glass and then settled into a cushioned chair and opened his bible. This bible contained the Apocryphal Gospels. Longinus turned to the Gospel of Nicodemus and began to read aloud in Greek.

"Then Longinus, a certain soldier, taking a spear, pierced his side, and …"

*Cursed,* he thought.

*Cursed to remain until the return of the man I killed.*

*But I didn't kill him, did I?*

*No. No I didn't kill him.*

*Jesus was destined to die.*

*Jesus was sent here to die.*

*Jesus Christ died to set all men free.*

*He died for love.*

Then Longinus turned to John 15:13 and read aloud.

"There is no greater love than this, that he lay down his life for his friends."

Longinus dropped the book and took his face in his hands. He began to weep.

# *CHAPTER SIX*

# *VAMPIRE*

The four-member People's Archeology Team were staying at the Park Hyatt Vienna Hotel on Innere Stadt near the Hofburg Palace. The Park Hyatt is located in Vienna's Golden Quarter, in a former bank building dating back to 1913. The hotel exudes luxury, taste, elegance, and most importantly — privacy. The four person team consisted of two male and two female counterintelligence members of the Chinese Ministry of State Security's Bureau #18. They had all been well-versed in the history of the Spear of Destiny by MSS archeologists, and their individual Professor of Archeology credentials, though fabricated, were impeccable. The team had smuggled into Austria with them an exact replica of the Longinus Spear to substitute. It had been artificially aged by technicians of their Operations Directorate. They were relying on the over willingness of the Hofburg officials for comradeship, and the very beguiled naivety of China-World relations to be able to pull the switch. All highly skilled counterintelligence operators, two members of the team had performed assassinations before. Tonight the team was dining inside the Hyatt Park Vienna Hotel at its delightfully charming Bank Brasserie Restaurant. Situating herself at the head of the table was team leader Nü Jiangshi. Next to her was her executive officer Ming Chen. They were flanked by the two male members of the team — Chong Zee and Wutu Shen. They were all in awe of the Hyatt, not entirely accustomed to being surrounded by such extravagant opulence and decadence.

"Captain James Ross, American, Special Forces," said Nü Jiangshi to her three colleagues at the table. "He's the one we must find."

The other three nodded in agreement to their boss.

"Yes," replied Ming Chen. "Ross is the key to this. He must be punished for the death of Admiral Shui Gui. He may even know the whereabouts of the machine known as Die Glocke."

"That is so," replied Nü Jiangshi. "For the next four days we will continue at the Hofburg with the Longinus Spear. They completely trust us ..."

"Perhaps they even fear us?" chimed in Wutu Shen.

"Perhaps," answered Nü Jiangshi. "And we will use that to our advantage."

Nü Jiangshi was thirty-one years old. Five-feet-nine-inches tall and weighing just under fifty kilograms, Nü had a toned athletic body from her years of military service and martial arts training. Her face was pale yet very sensual, with pouting full lips. Her silky black hair was cut in a trendy short bob with straight raven bangs to her wispy eyebrows. She was born and had grown up in the major industrial and commercial city of Wuhan, the capital city of Hubei Province in the

People's Republic of China. Her mother was a very beautiful woman from a traditional Buddhist Chinese agricultural family, and her father was a Lieutenant Colonel in the People's Army. Her uncle had died at Tiananmen Square, and since then her father had secretly studied Western philosophy and religion. Nü had gone to the prestigious Tsinghua University and majored in Marxist Theology. She married very young in college to her lover, a devoted communist theologian who cheated on her during her prolonged military service. Nü promptly divorced him, as the Communist Party celebrates divorce as an elegant approach to ending love, and praises it as a certificate of happiness. Becoming very bitter and resentful, Nü fully embraced communist indoctrination and propaganda. She promptly renounced her parents, and turned them in to the Communist Party for discipline. Nü's father and mother were sent to a Xinjiang concentration camp. Officially termed Vocational Education and Training Centers, the Xinjiang concentration camps are known for their extreme brutality. Several months after the most brutal camp indoctrination, Nü's mother was publicly and savagely raped by ten Chinese soldiers. Nü's father was forced to witness the rape, but he broke free and was killed trying to stop the attack. Since that time, Nü became bitterly cold hearted, ruthless, and a devoted disciple of Marxist-Leninist communist theology. Her name *Jiangshi* in the Mandarin language translates literally to *stiff walking corpse*. *Jiangshi* is a type of vampiric monster in ancient Chinese folklore. Said to be the result of the soul departing the body while energy still remains, the corpse moves around without any form of consciousness, feeling, or love. The Jiangshi kills by absorbing the victims *qi* or life force. It is literally a walking corpse, or vampire. Nü's nickname was Vamp. She had performed assassination before, and was personally hoping she would be the one to kill Captain Ross. That act would guarantee her next promotion. She trusted no one, especially the three sitting around the restaurant table with her. If she had to, Nü would betray her comrades to the Communist Party as effortlessly as she was tearing apart the warm bread in front of her.

A restaurant waiter arrived at their table bearing goblets of ice cold water and menus.

Nü carefully studied the menu.

"Wiener schnitzel with parsley potatoes, cucumber salad, and mountain cranberries," she said.

The waiter wrote it down on his little pad. "Would you care for a starter, mademoiselle?"

"A starter," said Nü, scanning the menu. "Yes. Yes I'll have a starter. French onion soup please."

The waiter wrote it down and looked around the table. The three others all ordered the exact same thing.

"Very good," replied the waiter, "excellent choice. Thank you," he said while bowing and then walked quickly towards the kitchen.

Nü leaned forward and spoke over the classical baroque music filtering in.

"But the way to a man is through his heart," said Jiangshi seductively raising her eyebrows. "This man Ross has a girlfriend. Her name is Lin Sparrow. If we get Lin Sparrow, then James Ross will fall."

The three members of the death squad stared intently at their leader.

“But do you really think Captain Ross and Miss Sparrow will come here, to us?” asked Chong Zee.

A cynical smile crept across Nü’s beautiful face.

“Our Pentagon assets tell us it is happening as we speak.”

The death squad members nodded their heads in finality.

# ***PART TWO***

*The impossible missions are the only ones that succeed.*

Jacques Cousteau
1910 — 1997
French Oceanographer

# *CHAPTER SEVEN*

# *CONTACT*

Ross's Samsung cellphone came to life.

*Bzzz.*

*Bzzz.*

*Bzzz.*

"What the —?"

Ross stared at the number. He immediately recognized it as having the 703 area code of Arlington Virginia.

*How in the hell?*

Ross remembered back to when he had thrown his US Army-issued Blackberry cellphone into the Limmat River in Zurich. That was after he had received a message on it to report back to the Warrior Transition Battalion at Fort Sam Houston Texas. Ross had been an inpatient convalescing there after the drone explosion which had incapacitated him. He had been ordered back because the US State Department reported that he had improperly used his diplomatic passport to enter Switzerland while on military leave — and they had turned him in.

*What to do?* thought Ross.

*What to do?*

Somehow the Department of Defense had been able to track him again, even though he was now using a secondhand Samsung Galaxy Stratosphere II that he had purchased from a local vendor in Berlin at the Tempelhof Park.

*Bzzz.*

*Bzzz.*

*Bzzz.*

The Samsung continued to ring.

Ross let out a string of obscenities.

"James, your language," laughed Lin playfully teasing.

Ross stood up and slowly walked away from the dining room table. He pushed the *accept call* button and took the call.

"Yeah?" he said.

There was a delay on the other end of the phone for a second.

"Hello?" said Ross.

"Jim Ross?" asked a voice.

"Is this Jim Ross?"

Ross immediately recognized the familiar voice.

"Yes sir," replied Ross.

"Jim this is Braxton," said the voice. "Braxton Matthews."

It was Ross's old Special Forces Battalion Commander, Braxton Matthews. General Matthews was now the Chief of Staff of the United States Army.

“Yes sir,” said Ross again.

“Jim, you’re not easy to get a hold of,” said Matthews. “I’ve been trying to contact you since last week. You must’ve been really busy.”

Ross had indeed been busy. But how could he explain to General Matthews that he had destroyed a Nazi time machine on the Bahamian Island of Abaco last week, and then time-traveled back to the Kecksburg Incident in 1965 to stop the rebirth of the Third Reich?

“Yes sir, a little busy,” explained Ross.

“Where are you now?” asked Matthews.

“Back in Zurich, sir. On leave. But I’ve been ordered back to Fort Sam Houston. Back to the Warrior Transition Battalion.”

“Why?” asked Matthews. “Listen, never mind, it doesn’t matter. I’ll take care of the WTB. Don’t worry about them. I’ve got explicit orders from the President. I’m going to send you a WARNO over the SIPRNet in the next five minutes. Do you have computer access?”

“Yes sir,” said Ross.

“Okay. How soon can you get to Vienna Austria?”

Ross knew the SIPRNet was the Department of Defense Secret Internet Protocol Router Network. And a warning order issued from General Matthews would be brief, but complete.

Ross thought about his plans to marry Lin. She was all he wanted in the world. He wanted to marry her and live the rest of his life with her. Perhaps they could even raise a family. Time after time his plans had been interrupted by duty — by fate. It appeared as if fate had yet again reared its ugly head and would interfere with those plans.

“I can be in Vienna tomorrow sir,” said Ross.

“Good,” said Matthews. “Now here’s what’s happening …”

# *CHAPTER EIGHT*

# *CHANGE OF PLANS*

Ross and General Matthews talked for well over an hour. When the call was over, Ross walked back into the dining room and sat down next to Lin. He reached out and held her hands in his.

"Let's go to our room," said Ross. "I've got to talk to you about something."

*Here it comes,* thought Lin.

*This is it.*

*I sensed it.*

*I dreamt it.*

*I know.*

They both stood up.

Holding hands, Ross and Lin slowly walked up the stairs and into their room.

Sitting down on the bed with Lin, Ross said, "I'm sorry Lin, but we're going to have to put the marriage plans on hold for a little bit more."

"Why? What's going on?" she asked.

Ross cleared his throat.

"Ah, evidently a Chinese Archeology Team is in Austria and is attempting to steal the Spear of Destiny …"

"What's the Spear of Destiny?" interrupted Lin.

Ross said, "Supposedly it's the spear that pierced the side of Christ at the crucifixion. Some people say it has magical powers."

Lin shuddered.

"Like what?" she asked.

"Umm, there are several myths attached to it. It is said to be able to heal the sick, bring victory in battles, and even foretell the future."

Lin started to feel a chill run up her back.

Ross said, "It has long been believed that armies which march behind the Spear of Destiny are invincible."

*My dream,* thought Lin. *It's exactly what my dream was about.*

"Well what does the Army expect you to do?"

Ross became deadly serious.

"That was part one. Part two is this Chinese Archeology Team is probably a cover for Chinese spies who may also be here about Die Glocke and what happened in the Bahamas last week."

Ross decided not to inform Lin about the alleged assassination plot against him.

Lin knew there was more to this.

"But why you? Why is the Army asking you to get involved? Why don't they send over someone else to deal with this?" asked Lin.

"Because I'm here," said Ross, "and close to Austria, and I know exactly what we're dealing with in regards to Die Glocke. No one else does. And General Matthews trusts me."

Lin thought about it a minute.

She knew there was more that Ross wasn't telling her. But she also knew it would do no good asking him. Ross was trying to protect her.

"That's why I have to go alone," said Ross.

Lin couldn't hide her astonishment.

"Alone? But why? Why alone? Surely you'll need help," pleaded Lin.

"I need you to stay back here with Die Glocke. You'll have to watch it, and make sure nothing happens to it," said Ross. "That machine can change the course of the world. It can alter history. And when I get back we'll need to destroy it. Listen Lin, this is a piece of cake. I'll reveal the Chinese Archeology Team as spies and turn over the information to the authorities. INTERPOL will make the arrest."

Lin thought for a second.

"So when do you leave?"

Ross looked at his battered Benrus Type I divers watch.

"Today. Lailani said I could take Emanuel's Mercedes-Benz in the garage. It takes about eight hours to drive to Vienna. And I'll need a car when I get there."

Lin leaned in forward and embraced Ross.

"All right my love," said Lin with tears welling in her eyes. "I'll wait here for you. I'll be here when you return."

Ross tenderly took Lin in his arms and laid her down on the bed. With his right hand he playfully brushed her silky dark brown hair off her forehead. Looking into her almond eyes, Ross saw his future, his life, his very destiny. He closed his eyes, tilted his head, and kissed her. Lin's lips were full, and soft, and warm. She responded to the kiss by wrapping her arms around his neck and pulling him to her. Her scent was like an aphrodisiac to Ross. He kissed her again, only this time more tenderly. Lin's body quivered under his embrace. Lin unbuttoned Ross's shirt as he undid her skirt. Soon all their clothes were on the floor in a jumbled mass.

Lin's sensuous nude body folded together with Ross's muscled and hardened torso. His chest brushed across her erect nipples, further adding fuel to his already consuming desire. She smiled and played with Ross's hair for a few seconds, twisting and turning it in her fingers. She tried to brush it off his forehead, but it just fell back down again only in more disarray. Then Lin rolled over on top of Ross's body. She blossomed around him. Ross stiffened, and Lin threw her head back and rocked her hips, grasping Ross's chest with both hands. She arched her back and rocked her hips again and again. Lin gaspingly moaned during the sweet rhythmic gyrations, and perspiration started to gather on both their foreheads. Then she suddenly fell forward on top of Ross's chest. Their lips explored each other passionately, shamelessly, and unendingly. Their movements flowed like a powerful current in the sea, ever smoothly and increasing, until the undulations of the swell crested and crashed into the shore in all its majesty in a burst of brilliant warm colors.

# *CHAPTER NINE*

# *SPQR*

Lailani gave Ross the keys and he started up the Mercedes. The black 1972 Mercedes-Benz S-Class was Emanuel's taxi. It was a four door luxury sedan which had a 6.9 liter V8 engine, anti-lock brakes, self-leveling heavy duty suspension, black leather seats, six-CD changer, Sirus satellite radio, and GPS system. Every time Ross ever sat in the car he was immediately overtaken by the aroma of roses. It reminded Ross of the centuries old Christian tradition that the smell of roses when none are around is a sign that an angel may be communicating with you.

Emanuel Mesiyas was young, and appeared to be in his early thirties, perhaps thirty-three. He had a medium frame, and stood at around five-feet-ten-inches tall. His smooth dark skin immediately reminded Ross of a full blooded Filipino. His black hair was clean and neatly groomed, shoulder length, and parted in the middle. The man always looked as if he hadn't shaved in a week or two. He smiled easily and displayed pearly white teeth. His eyes were dark brown and reassuringly gentle. His face had a strange glow about it that immediately put Ross at ease. Emanuel was the enigmatic taxicab driver who Ross had originally met on Operation CAPACITY STRIKE in the Philippines. He had flown Ross through a severe typhoon, and stood side-by-side with him during a bloody firefight with Abu-Sayyaf terrorists. Emanuel further assisted Ross on Operation TIMELESS TERROR in Zurich, in which Ross destroyed the financial empire of international terrorist Wolfram von Lugoff. Lin Sparrow had been killed at the end of that mission, but with the help of Emanuel and his Mossad friends, Ross enacted his revenge and used Die Glocke to literally travel back in time to save her life. And last week in the Bahamas during Operation TIMELESS EMBRACE, Emanuel had saved Lin's life and killed the sadistic Chinese Admiral Shui Gui, while helping Ross destroy two of the original three Nazi Die Glocke time machines.

Inside the Mercedes, Ross set the GPS to the Hofburg Palace in Vienna. He drove the sedan out of the garage and soon was passing the Bahnhofquai. Ross drove over the Limmat River by way of the Walchebrücke, and continued on to Walchestrasse. It was an eight hour trip no matter how Ross cut it. He just had to settle back and drive.

Ross noticed the Mercedes had a six-CD changer. He popped it out and started looking through the musical choices. One CD had Ross's name written across it in big red letters.

*Curious,* he thought. *I wonder what this is?*

Ross pressed the CD cartridge into the changer and selected the disc marked JAMES ROSS. He turned up the sound.

"James, this is Emanuel," said the voice on the CD.

Ross immediately recognized his old friend's voice.

"If you're listening to this, then you are on your way to the Hofburg Palace."

Ross was shocked.

"Which means Lailani let you drive my car, so be careful with it."

Ross smiled to himself.

"I can't be with you physically on this mission, but I'll be with you in spirit. So, you're on your way to safeguard the Spear of Destiny. I know you understand the legend of the spear, and its historical significance. Watch your back my friend. Be alert. There are forces in this world that wish to enslave it. I'm sorry I don't have any members of Mossad to offer you on this mission. But, I do have an ally for you. His name is Inus — Lon G. Inus. He's a friend of mine. I've known Lon for many, many years. He's sort of an unofficial protector of the Holy Lance. I don't have a picture to give you, but I can provide a pretty good description: Lon is thirty-four years old. He's six-foot-two, and weighs 187 pounds. His hair is cut short and shiny black. Lon is Italian and always looks suntanned, and he is extremely fit. He used to be a soldier, a captain. He dresses much like you in dark clothes. One feature you can't miss is his eyes. They are dark brown, probing, and with a touch of melancholy. I've been told he kinda resembles a young Sylvester Stallone. Oh, one other thing — Lon has a tattoo on his left forearm — SPQR. How do you get in touch with him? Lon always has lunch weekdays at noon at Le Salzgries, a

French restaurant on number six Marc Aurel Strasse, in Vienna. I hear the French Onion soup is delicious. That's it my friend. My prayers and best wishes go with you always. Take care of yourself James."

The CD ended.

Ross was mesmerized.

*Emanuel knew this was going to happen,* he thought.

*He knew I would be driving his car and on this particular mission.*

*But how?*

*How did he know?*

Ross searched his memory.

*SPQR?*

Ross knew what the acronym stood for.

*Senatus Populusque Romanus.*

*The Senate and the People of Rome.*

*The Roman Empire.*

"Ah-huh," said Ross to himself.

"Curious tattoo."

Ross arrived in Vienna at midnight. He decided to use his issued GSA (US Government Services Administration) visa card.

*What the hell,* thought Ross. *I'm on orders from the President. I've got a copy in my pocket.*

Ross smiled to himself.

*Shouldn't the President's representative be comfortable?*

He thought about the commander of the Warrior Transition Battalion back at Fort Sam Houston.

*That guy must be pulling his hair out.*

Ross checked his GPS for hotels and decided to stop at the Herrenhof Steigenberger Hotel at 10 Herrengasse, Innere Stadt. The Steigenberger is right in the heart of the 1st District, and an easy walk to the Hofburg Palace. Surrounded by restaurants, shopping, the opera, parliament, and the government quarter, the Steigenberger is a classic example of old world grace, charm, and sophistication.

Ross checked in and was given room 323.

The concierge raised his arm and snapped his fingers.

Immediately, a teenaged male porter shuffled up to Ross.

The porter was wearing white slacks, white shoes, and a white Victorian Renaissance jacket. The man bowed and reached down picking up Ross's bag.

Ross read his name tag which listed his name as Sebastian.

The porter led Ross to a bank of elevators. He pressed the *UP* button and the elevator doors hissed open. The porter selected the third floor button on the control panel and looked at Ross.

"Will you be staying with us long, sir?" inquired the porter.

"Perhaps a week," said Ross.

The elevator stopped at the third floor and the doors slid open.

Ross followed the teenaged porter down the long expanse of plush red carpeted hallway to room 323.

The porter slipped the electronic coded plastic card key into its slot. The small door lock light switched from red to green with an audible *click.* Pulling the card out, the porter opened the door and gave Ross a tour of his room.

"We have every conceivable amenity available here, sir," said the porter. "Secure computer access, luxury spas with massage therapy, fully equipped exercise rooms, a magnificent indoor heated swimming pool, and world class restaurants."

"Anything you could possibly need, sir," said the porter smiling.

Ross said, "Thank you Sebastian," and pressed a ten dollar American bill into the man's hands.

The porter bowed deeply and quickly shuffled out of the room closing the door behind him.

Ross threw his bag on the bed. He walked over to the room's complimentary Lenovo laptop computer and logged onto the internet. Ross accessed the Department of Defense Secret Internet Protocol Router Network to send his emails. He typed a personal encrypted email to General Matthews:

Sir,

Arrived Vienna midnight local time.

Morning site survey planned.

Updates to follow.

v/r

CPT James B. Ross

*That was enough for now*, he thought.

Ross pressed the send button and the message was gone through secure SIPRNet channels. He logged off of the Lenovo computer and closed the laptop lid.

Ross leaned over and picked up the receiver of the desk phone and pressed the wakeup service button.

He asked for a wakeup call at six o'clock in the morning.

The soft demure voice of the female receptionist purred, "Certainly sir, and have a very pleasant evening Mister Ross."

"Thank you, Ma'am," replied Ross.

He laid the receiver back in its cradle.

Noticing a bank of electric outlets on the desk near the phone, Ross plugged his cellphone into one for charging.

Next, he opened his suitcase and hung his black suit in the closet, and stowed the rest of his clothes in the draws of the dresser next to the widescreen Samsung television.

Ross walked into the bathroom and stripped off his clothes and threw them down. He loaded his toothbrush with hotel courtesy toothpaste and methodically brushed the staleness of eight hours worth of travel out of his mouth. Glancing in the mirror and fingering the stubble on his chin, Ross decided to shave in the morning. He walked to the bathroom and slid open the twin transparent glass doors of the shower stall and stepped in. Twisting the crystal power jet handles counterclockwise, he straightened out his arms and leaned forward, pressing both of his palms against the shower wall under the needling spray. Ross lowered his head and allowed the heavy stream of pulsating hot water to cascade over his aching body.

Ross completed the shower in his usual four minutes. He grabbed one of the large blue terrycloth towels and dried himself off. Then he put on a pair of green plaid boxer shorts and crawled under the crisp bed sheets.

Sleep came quickly, and his dreams were filled with vampires, walking corpses, and death.

# *CHAPTER TEN*

# *LON G. INUS*

Ross awoke with the jolt of an electric spark.

It was ten minutes before six o'clock in the morning.

As usual, he had mentally impelled himself to wake up through sheer force of will before receiving the hotel's courtesy wakeup telephone call.

Ross staggered into the bathroom, flicking on the lights and fan.

He turned on the shower and stepped in, not wasting any time.

In three minutes his shower was over.

Ross stepped out of the shower stall and wrapped one of the huge blue terrycloth hotel towels around his waist.

Wiping his right hand across the steam covered mirror, he looked at himself. He fingered his mornings worth of stubble and reached for his AAFES shave gel. With a liberal amount of Army-Air-Force-Exchange-Services shave gel on, he slowly glided his razor across his face. He lowered his head towards the sink and splashed hot water across his face to rinse off the remaining residue. Finally, he poured Aqua Velva Ice Blue aftershave into his cupped left hand and slapped it on his face.

*Now that is refreshing.*

Ross walked to the closet and pulled out his black suit.

He dressed quickly.

Highlighting his suit was a white cotton shirt with a narrow black necktie. Finishing the four-in-hand knot, he cinched up the necktie to his collar.

He ran his hand through his hair to try and push it off his forehead, but it just fell back down again.

Ross went to his bag and pulled out a Beretta 71 .22LR pistol. It was the same gun Emanuel had given him from his Mossad friends. He brought three loaded magazines with him. Ross slid one into the butt of the Beretta and racked the slide back chambering a round. He flicked up the Beretta's safety. Then he placed the weapon and extra magazines in the complimentary room safe and set the combination.

Ross glanced at himself in the mirror. Satisfied, he snatched up his wallet and keys, strapped on his Benrus, and walked out of the room closing the door behind him.

*It's only a ten minute walk to Le Salzgries Restaurant,* thought Ross as he headed for the elevator. He rode the elevator down and walked out through the front double doors of the Steigenberger. A gust of frigid air hit him, and Ross turned up his suit collar and thrust his hands into his pockets. Outside in front of the hotel was an elegant complimentary horse drawn carriage.

*Straight out of Cinderella,* he thought.

Ross sauntered down Herrengasse Strasse, taking in the sights. The morning was vibrantly alive with red and green twinkling Christmas lights everywhere. Long silver strands of tinsel were strung across lamp posts giving them a chandelier-type appearance. Frosted merchant shop windows displayed everything from electronic toys to the latest designer fashions. An ocean of taxis were beeping their horns and zooming in and out of storefront parking. Couples were engulfed by the sights and sounds of the Viennese holiday season. Their breath was coming out in puffs as one, circling and disappearing skyward as they huddled closer, arm-in-arm, with smiles on their faces. It was the hustle and bustle of the merriest time of year in Austria. It was a scene reminiscent of a Charles Dickens novel.

Small gusts of wind carrying wet flakes of snow swirled around and teased at Ross. He stopped in front of a shop window displaying wedding dresses and tuxedos.

Ross pressed his left thumb and forefinger to the bridge of his nose and squeezed, tightly closing his eyes. He shook his head and tried to clear his mind of all thoughts — except Lin.

Her passionate embrace would quench his fiery temper.

Her gentle eyes would soothe his wounded heart.

Her soft lips would calm his restless spirit.

Her unconditional love would rescue his tortured soul.

Lin Sparrow was all that James Ross would ever require.

Falling in love with her was like a miracle.

She was a bright light that illuminated his life.

He found the best aspects of himself in the presence of Lin.

His marriage plans to Lin had been put off because of orders.

*But this was different,* thought Ross.

*This was the Spear of Destiny.*

*If the Chinese gain control of it, they would have absolute power.*

*Communist Chinese armies would march over the face of the earth.*

*I've got to stop it.*

*I've got to safeguard the spear.*

*I hated lying to Lin.*

*But if she knew I was in danger, no one would be able to stop her from being here.*

*And I couldn't face losing Lin again.*

Ross looked at his Benrus Type I. Its blade-type hands told him it was 1155.

*Le Salzgries Restaurant should be right around the corner,* he thought.

No sooner had he rounded the corner than he caught sight of Le Salzgries Restaurant at number 6 Marc Aurel Strasse.

Ross checked both ways for traffic and then hurried across the street, dodging taxis as he went. He stepped onto the restaurant's front stoop and pulled open the heavy glass door. Walking inside, Ross was immediately greeted by headwaiter Günter.

"Good afternoon Mein Herr. And how are you this fine day?" asked Günter.

Günter looked to be in his early forties. He was wearing an older style dark blue Armani suit with inch-and-a-half lapels, and a Bellamy white laced Victorian shirt. His collar was open and he had it accented by a Gusleson dark burgundy floral ascot. Standing at six-foot-two and weighing two hundred pounds, Günter was stout and had the broken nose of a boxer. His head was completely shaven, and he sported a large drooping dark brown mustache.

"Fine, fine," answered Ross.

"One for lunch today, Mein Herr?" asked Günter.

"Ah yes, but I'm looking for someone," replied Ross scanning the restaurant.

Günter raised a curious eyebrow.

"Perhaps I may be of service, Mein Herr?"

Ross said, "His name is Mister Inus. Lon Inus."

"Aber natürlich," replied Günter. "Herr Inus is a regular here. Allow me to take you to his table. Ah, what is your name Mein Herr?"

"James Ross."

Günter nodded and motioned for Ross to follow. He led him through the packed lunchtime crowd to a far side corner table in the smoking section.

"Pardon me Herr Inus," said Günter. "May I present Herr James Ross."

Ross stood there for a second and sized up Inus.

*He's exactly how Emanuel described him,* Ross thought. *Right down to the dark suit.*

Lon Inus immediately stood up. He stretched out his hand to Ross. The handshake was firm and friendly.

"Pleased to make your acquaintance James," said Inus.

Günter saw that everything was okay so he bowed and excused himself away.

"Here's my card. Please have a seat," said Inus.

"Thank you," said Ross.

Ross pocketed the card and pulled out a chair, and then sat down. Both men smiled at each other.

"I believe we have a mutual friend in Emanuel Mesiyas," said Ross, attempting to break the ice.

"Yes that is correct," answered Inus. "How long have you known Emanuel?"

"Let's see," said Ross shifting his gaze to the ceiling. "I guess about a little less than a year." Ross returned his gaze to Inus. "How long have you known him?"

Inus smiled and replied, "Considerably longer."

Ross picked up a glass of ice water from the table and took a sip.

"Have you been to Vienna before?" asked Inus.

"No, never. This is my first visit."

"It's a beautiful city. Very historical, and rich in culture and tradition," said Inus, "lots of tradition."

Ross picked up a menu.

"What do you recommend here?"

Inus said, "Just about everything is good. I like the steaks. But the shrimp is great, so is the lobster."

Inus raised his arm and snapped his fingers. A blonde waitress scurried over to the table.

"May I take your order please?" she said.

Nineteen-year-old Brigitte Arnré had been a waitress at Le Salzgries for the past eight months. Brigitte was a native of Innsbruck and working as a waitress to pay for her philosophy degree from the University of Vienna. Today she was wearing a purple Shein Vcay dress with square neck and shirred waist ruffle hem. The dress was tight across her breasts and low in the back. It was cinched to her waist by a two-inch-wide black leather belt with silver baroque buckle. Her feet were nestled in three-inch-heeled black baroque shoes resplendent with matching silver baroque buckles. Her blonde hair was in twin French braids with tiny thin curls reaching to her eyebrows. Her beautiful face was reminiscent of a young Kim Basinger. Brigitte wore purple lipstick with a wet gloss to accent her sensuous mouth. Her fingernails were cut short and painted gloss highland green. She smelled of Florecita eau de parfum. Brigitte radiated a healthy, fun-loving, joyful ambience.

Inus said, "Yes, I'll have the filet mignon, medium, with haricots verts and a salad."

Brigitte wrote it down on her little pad.

"What salad dressing would you like?" she asked.

"Um, Italian please," answered Inus.

"And to drink?"

"Bring me a tall Märzenbier," said Inus.

Brigitte turned her attention to Ross.

"And for you?"

Ross had asked the next question at dozens of restaurants around the world. He enjoyed the routine and loved the responses. Mostly though, he loved the soup.

"Do you have French onion soup today?" inquired Ross.

Brigitte looked up from her notepad and smiled.

"Why yes sir. The best French onion soup in the whole of Vienna," she said proudly.

"Okay. I'll have French onion soup, with a large thin slice of cheese melted over the top," said Ross returning her smile. "And I would like the bacon wrapped filet, medium, with green beans, and a salad with thousand island dressing. And bring me a Märzenbier too."

Brigitte smiled back and looked at Inus, raising her eyebrows.

"Give me the French onion soup as well," said Inus smiling. "I don't think I can pass that up."

Ross gathered the menus and handed them to Brigitte.

She smiled and walked away, but the scent of her perfume lingered.

Both men sipped their water while their eyes followed Brigitte's departure.

"Okay," said Inus, placing both of his hands flat on the table and looking at Ross. "How can I help you James?"

Ross cleared his throat.

"Ah, Emanuel told me you're sort of an unofficial protector of the spear — the Spear of Destiny?"

Inus reached inside his suit pocket and pulled out his Muratti Ambassador brand cigarettes. He tapped the packet with the crook of his left forefinger and extracted one.

Ross immediately pulled out his Zippo lighter and stretched his arm across the table. He popped open the top and flicked the thumbwheel downward, igniting a wavering bluish flame.

Inus eyed Ross and leaned his face in to permit Ross to light his Muratti. He cocked his head to the side and allowed himself the luxury of a long, slow draw. The Centurian held the smoke in his lungs for a moment, and then tilted his head upwards hissing the tobacco vapors out through his nostrils.

"Thank you," said Inus. "The Spear of Destiny? Yes, over the years I've become sort of a protector I imagine. I understand its history and believe in its capabilities. Why do you ask?"

Ross said, "I'm here for the same reason — to protect the spear."

"Is there another threat against it?" asked Inus.

"Of a sort, yes. I've been sent here by my government. We've recently come into possession of information detailing a Chinese attempt to substitute the original spear with a replica."

Inus thought for a second.

"Really. When is this supposed to take place?" he asked.

Just then Brigitte returned with a tray load of food. She placed the French onion soups and steaks in front of them, along with their Märzenbiers.

"Be careful gentlemen, the plates are very hot," gushed Brigitte.

"Thank you," said Ross.

As Brigitte left, Inus said, "I'm looking forward to this soup."

Ross picked up his knife and fork to cut his steak when he quickly noticed Inus had bowed his head in prayer.

Inus prayed silently.

*God, allow me to help this young man in his quest. Deliver us from the evil one, and protect us in battle. In the name of your holy son Jesus, I ask this, amen.*

Ross gently put down his utensils and bowed his head.

Inus observed Ross's gesture.

"I visit the Holy Lance everyday," said Inus. "I check on it. I am more than happy to provide you with all my expertise as needed to safeguard the spear."

"Thank you. I'll need it," said Ross.

"I understand you're a soldier in the American Army?" queried Inus.

"Yes, yes I am."

"And are you still on active duty," asked Inus.

"Yes," answered Ross between mouthfuls. "Emanuel tells me you were a soldier as well?"

Inus's face took on a faraway look.

"Yes," he replied, "but it was a long time ago."

The two soldiers turned their concentration to their lunch.

# *CHAPTER ELEVEN*

# *HOFBURG PALACE*

After lunch, Inus led Ross over to the Hofburg Imperial Palace Museum.

"I think you will find the museum quite fascinating," said Inus.

They entered and had to go through a metal detector. Ross had to place his keys and lighter into the security bin to pass through. A security guard then handed the items back to Ross.

"Thank you sir," said the guard.

The Hofburg Palace covers an area of over 240,000 square meters. It includes multiple buildings, squares, courtyards and gardens. Inus took Ross on a guided tour. He pointed out the most notable treasures including the Habsburg imperial crown of the Holy Roman Emperor, the solid gold rosebush, the crown jewels, the coronation robes, and the fifteenth century sword of Emperor Maximilian. Soon they were in front of the display case protecting the Holy Lance.

"This is it James," said Inus.

Ross stared at the ancient spear in the case. It actually was only the head of the spear without its long shaft. He guessed it was approximately eighteen inches long and about two inches in diameter. It was held together by wire wound along its length at various intervals, and in the middle by what appeared to be folded sheets of gold. Ross could see two small crosses etched on the top portion of the blade, and two more small crosses etched on each fin holding the blade to the remnants of the shaft.

"What is that written on the gold portion?" asked Ross.

Inus leaned in to explain.

"It says *Lancea et Clavvs Domini*."

Ross looked at Inus.

"That means *Lance and Nail of the Lord*," said Inus. "What you see wrapped towards the tip there by wire is one of the iron nails that was hammered into Christ."

Suddenly an electric shock flowed through Ross's body.

"Jesus," said Ross.

"Yes that's right," replied Inus.

Ross noticed a white placard on the side of the display case. It read:

DISPLAY TO BE CLOSED AFTERNOONS
TO ALLOW ARCHEOLOGICAL STUDY

Ross looked at Inus.

"That could be it," whispered Inus.

The pair turned to continue their tour when the Chinese People's Archeology Team walked in and immediately surrounded the display case. They were all there — Ming Chen, Chong Zee, Wutu Shen, and Nü Jiangshi.

"Magnificent isn't it?" said Nü.

The other three team members all nodded their heads in agreement.

Ross and Inus turned around and looked at them.

"I said magnificent isn't it?" repeated Nü staring at Ross.

Ross and Inus looked at Nü.

Nü was dressed in a red Chinese cheongsam dress. The dress was split at the right side all the way up to her smooth thigh, with tiny gold embroidered buttons lining the left side up to the two-inch-high Mandarin neck collar. A design of an embroidered golden dragon enticingly crawled across her bosom. Her short trimmed fingernails and toenails were painted gloss black. She wore four-inch high heeled black open-toed shoes, and no stockings. Her sassy black hair was cut in a trendy short bob with straight black bangs above the very dark brown pools of her eyes. Her lips pouted with a very wet pink colored lip gloss, and her broad cheeks had been brushed with rouge powder.

"Yes," said Ross. "Magnificent."

Nü's sadistic soulless eyes absorbed every inch of James Ross.

*So this is the American assassin?* thought Nü.

*Two of them.*

*How very interesting.*

Ross stared back at Nü. Pinned above her proud left breast was a small white tag announcing — Visitor Pass, Chinese Team.

Inus looked at Ross and tapped his 1940 Eterna chronograph wristwatch.

"Time for us to be going," said Inus.

Ross nodded.

He brushed past Nü and static electricity snapped through both of them.

"It seems we've got a connection," purred Nü, batting her eyes and flirting as demurely and sensuously as she could.

Ross turned to her and smiled.

"Clearly," he said.

Ross and Inus walked out of the exhibit and down the hall.

Ming Chen turned to Nü and said, "That was the American, James Ross, wasn't it?"

"Yes."

Ming cinched up her petite nose quizzically.

"Who was that with him?"

Nü shrugged her shoulders.

"I do not know. He must be an ally. Perhaps he is CIA, or even Army Intelligence."

Both women stared at the spear through the display case.

"Ross is quite handsome, isn't he?" asked Ming.

"Yes."

"So is the other one," said Ming.

"Yes they both are," answered Nü. "But orders are orders. We will take care of them after we have secured the spear. Nothing will stop us from completing our task," said Nü.

Ming reached out and held hands with Nü.

"Their deaths will bring glory to the People's Republic," said Ming.

*You stupid little girl,* thought Nü. *You are so naive.*

"Ross is mine," snarled Nü. "Do not touch him. You can have the other one."

Ming Chen blushed.

"Certainly Commander, certainly," said Ming.

*This may turn out yet to be an enjoyable assignment,* Nü thought. *A real labor of love.*

# *CHAPTER TWELVE*

# *ALLIES*

Once outside Ross and Inus crossed the square and decided to stop at a small Viennese coffee shop.

"Sit anywhere you like," said the waiter behind the bar. The waiter looked like a young version of Johnny Depp wearing a white apron.

Inus motioned Ross over to a table and pulled out a chair.

"You've got to try Vienna's world famous Melange coffee," he said while sitting down.

"Okay," said Ross taking a seat, "that sounds great."

Inus raised his hand to the waiter.

"Two Melange coffees please."

"Bien sûr," replied the waiter.

"That was all four of them," said Inus.

"Yeah," replied Ross. "A four person team, two men and two women. The leader must be the woman who spoke. It's been my experience with communist militaries that only the leader will speak."

*Not too different than the Legions,* thought Inus to himself.

The waiter approached the table and placed down two coffees and two waters.

"Here you go sir. I'm Jett. If you need anything else just let me know."

"Thank you Jett," replied Inus.

Jett bowed and excused himself.

"So what is Melange coffee exactly?" asked Ross.

"Well," explained Inus, "it's an espresso but with steamed milk, and topped with foamed cream."

"Kinda like what we would call a cappuccino?" asked Ross.

"Yes, somewhat," replied Inus, "but we use a little less milk. The water is a palate cleanser to use between sips so you can savor the flavor more."

Ross took a sip of the coffee.

"Hey, that's great stuff," said Ross.

Inus smiled.

"The switch has not taken place yet," said Inus.

Ross took another sip of his Melange coffee and raised an eyebrow.

"How do you know that?"

Inus slowly stirred a teaspoon of sugar into his coffee. His eyes started to glaze over.

"The wire that is used to bind the nail to the cross …"

Ross stared at Inus.

*What's wrong with the guy? He seems to have drifted into another world, another time,* thought Ross.

"… I mean, the wire holding the nail has developed a certain patina that has evolved over two thousand years. It has never been successfully duplicated by any counterfeiter."

"You mean duplicates have been created before?" asked Ross.

"Yes, quite a number of them, but for legitimate purposes. Certain collectors, religious organizations, and museums will pay for a replica to be made, and they leave no doubt to be had that it is in fact a replica," said Inus.

"That's what the Chinese want everyone to believe here," said Ross. "They are supposed to be making a replica for their National Museum in Beijing."

"I see," said Inus.

"Where do you think the switch will take place?" asked Ross.

Inus thought for a second.

"So if I were going to make a switch it would be in the Hofburg restoration workshop," said Inus. "And I would already have a replica with me."

"They do," said Ross. "Supposedly they brought one in country with them, and the fear and respect commanded by President Xi Jinping is such that their archeology team was simply waved through customs."

*Absolutely reminds me of the corrupt power of the Senate of Rome,* thought Inus.

"We'll have to intercept the spear outside the Hofburg museum then," said Ross.

Ross took another sip of his Melange coffee.

"Make no mistake Lon, the Chinese are dangerous. The entire team is composed of members of their Ministry of State Security, which means they are trained intelligence assets, and totally dedicated to communism," said Ross.

Lon Inus looked Ross straight in the eyes.

"Do you believe?"

Ross leaned forward in his chair.

"Believe in what?" asked Ross.

Inus cleared his throat.

"James, do you believe in the power of the spear?" he asked.

Ross thought for a second.

*I've seen many strange things in this world,* thought Ross. *I know for a fact the Nazi time machine Die Glocke exists and is real. I even believe I saw Emanuel vanish from the seat of a German Horten 229 V9 flying wing just last week.*

"Umm, if it's the real Spear of Destiny, then yeah, I believe," said Ross.

Inus smiled and looked satisfied.

"The spear is a reminder to all of us that the power of the Divine is real. If the spear should fall into the wrong hands, as it did in World War Two, then the forces of darkness can march over the face of the earth."

Ross studied Inus.

"We cannot let the Holy Lance fall into the hands of China," said Inus.

"We won't," replied Ross.

He looked at his Benrus. Its blade-type hands told him it was 1535 hours.

"I need to find out what hotel the Chinese Team is staying at," said Ross.

Inus said matter-of-factly, "They are at the Park Hyatt Hotel on Innere Stadt near the Hofburg Palace, in the Golden Quarter."

A look of surprise spread across Ross's face as he sat back in the chair.

"How do you know that?" said Ross.

Then Ross thought, *It doesn't really matter how this guy knows. He obviously has his secrets, but then so do I.*

"Are you sure?" asked Ross.

"Yes. All four of them," said Inus.

"What else can you share about them?" asked Ross.

Ross grabbed a napkin and started writing on it.

Inus said, "The two women are Nü Jiangshi and Ming Chen."

Ross wrote on the napkin.

"The men are Wutu Shen and Chong Zee. They have all been here for two days."

"Do you have any idea when they are planning to leave?" asked Ross.

"I believe it will be the day after tomorrow. That means we've got two days to stop them," said Inus.

Ross finished taking notes and folded the napkin in half. He stuck it in his suit coat pocket.

*I wonder where this guy gets his information?* thought Ross, *because it's more detailed than what I got from General Matthews.*

*How does he know these things? Why does he have the names of the Chinese Team? How does he know what hotel they're staying at? And this guy is a friend of Emanuel's? Emanuel was one of those guys who you met and you just knew you could trust him. Lin thought he was an angel. Emanuel told her he could see an aura around her, and that people are brought into our lives for a reason. This guy Inus, Lon G. Inus, he's like Emanuel. He seems to know a lot of esoteric stuff. Wait a minute —*

Ross pulled out the napkin and wrote on it.

LON G. INUS

LONGINUS

"I can take you over to their hotel if you wish James," said Inus.

Ross refolded the napkin and put it away.

"Yeah," said Ross. "That'll be great."

# *CHAPTER THIRTEEN*

# *FIRST STRIKE*

The Asiatisches Essen Philippine Restaurant was very busy tonight. Lailani and her two waitresses were taking orders, and her husband Lars was overseeing the kitchen staff. The restaurant was overflowing with the smells of exotic food, the clatter of pots and pans, and the chatter of couples enjoying a night on the town. All this was blended together with the overhead Christmas music. Lin Sparrow had spent the afternoon putting up the Christmas tree and decorations, and was now dividing her time trying to help out wherever she could.

Just after dusk four men entered the restaurant. Lailani noticed them first. They were well-groomed and dressed in dark suits. They all appeared to be in their late twenties, extremely fit, and with hair slightly longer than that normally found on soldiers.

"Yitzhak!" yelled Lailani with a look of surprise on her face. She ran over and gave the man a big hug and kissed him on the cheek. The men were all friends of hers — Yitzhak Zanir, Shabtai Yatom, Benjamin Shiloah, and Zvi Harel.

"Shabtai, Benjamin, and Zvi!" said Lailani excitedly as she hugged and kissed all the men. "Welcome! Welcome!"

"I didn't know you were coming," said Lailani. "What are you doing here?"

Zanir said teasingly, "It's been way too long since we've seen you. We've come for great food, and to visit you, and for business."

Smiling, Lailani said, "Come on."

She led them all over to a table.

"Here you go, have a seat. I'll get Lars and ..."

"Lailani," said Zanir, "is James Ross still here?"

Lailani looked at Zanir quizzically.

"No. He's gone on to Austria. But why do you ask?"

"We need to talk to him tonight," said Zanir.

Lailani thought for a second.

"Well, his fiancée Lin is here. I'm sure she would be more than happy to talk to you," said Lailani trying to be helpful.

Zanir nodded. "Okay. It's quite important."

Lailani's eyes searched the restaurant for Lin. She saw her coming out of the kitchen with a tray of food.

"Let me get her for you," said Lailani.

Lailani walked over and talked to Lin. Then she led Lin over to the table with the four young men.

"Lin, let me introduce you to my very good and trusted friends — Yitzhak Zanir, Shabtai Yatom, Benjamin Shiloah, and Zvi Harel."

"Hello," said Lin.

Zanir immediately stood up and offered Lin a seat. “Here Lin, please sit down with us.”

Lin sat down at the table and looked into the faces of the team of men.

“The team” consisted of four Israeli men. All of the men had served previously in the IDF (Israeli Defense Forces) Special Forces units. Now, they were members of Mossad.

*Mossad* is a Hebrew word, translated into English as *The Institute.* Their entire title is The Institute for Intelligence and Special Operations. Mossad is the national intelligence agency of Israel, much like the CIA is for the United States. Mossad’s primary missions include: intelligence collection, operations, and counterterrorism. The men Lin had just been introduced to had been operating out of the Israeli consulate in Zurich. Mossad reports directly to the Prime Minister of Israel.

Yitzhak Zanir was the youngest of the men, and was the Kidon commissioned team leader. He studied Lin for a few seconds.

“Lin,” said Zanir, “we've worked in the past with Emanuel and James.”

“I know,” said Lin. “James told me about it. You guys have similar goals. James is in Vienna right now. But why are you here?”

Zanir looked at his men and then back at Lin.

“We’ve come for the machine. The machine that James and Emanuel brought back with them from Berlin.”

*Die Glocke. They want Die Glocke.* thought Lin.

Lin remembered that James had wanted her to watch over Die Glocke until his return, and then they were going to destroy it.

"What for?" asked Lin.

Shabtai Yatom spoke up quickly as if irritated.

"That's classified," said Yatom.

Zanir held up his hand and interrupted him.

"What he means is, we need to get a hold of the machine so it doesn't fall into the wrong hands. I'm sure you can understand that?"

"Yes I understand that," said Lin. "Emanuel and James didn't want it to fall into the wrong hands either. Why do you think it will? Is there an active plan from someone to steal it?"

Zanir nodded to Zvi Harel.

"Yes Lin, as a matter of fact we have reports that a Chinese team may be searching for the machine right now," said Harel, "and no one wants the Chinese to have that kind of mechanism."

The talking stopped as Lailani arrived at the table and placed down a tray of food and drinks. There were plates of sizzling sliced veal with dark brown gravy, shredded golden fried potatoes, green salads with rich vinaigrette dressing, and hot buttered bread rolls. Lailani also placed a pitcher of iced tea and a pitcher of San Miguel beer on the table.

"Nothing beats Philippine beer," she said. "Enjoy."

No sooner had Lailani delivered the food than the front door opened yet again. A blustery burst of frigid December air sprinkled with snowflakes swirled through the entranceway as three people hurried inside.

The Mossad team and Lin turned to watch as three Chinese men entered the Asiatisches Essen Philippine Restaurant. Lailani scurried over and after a brief discussion led them to a nearby table.

Zanir continued with his meal.

"Sir," said Benjamin Shiloah, "that's them. That's the Chinese team we've been trying to keep ahead of. Somehow they found out about this location."

Zanir glanced up from his plate at the Chinese men.

"Don't be alarmed Lin," said Zanir. "Chinese intelligence are some of the best in the world. I don't believe they will cause a ruckus here. They are strictly observing, fact finding."

"Lin," said Zanir between bites, "is it here?"

Lin realized there was not much she could do now.

*These Mossad guys want Die Glocke,* she thought. *And now it looks like the Chinese want it as well.*

"It's in the garage out back," said Lin.

Zanir nodded.

"Okay," he said. "Zvi and Shabtai, go out back and secure the garage."

The men excused themselves to Lin and promptly left the table.

Lin studied Zanir for a second. Her instincts told her that he was someone she could trust.

"James is in Austria on account of the Chinese," said Lin.

Zanir stopped eating and reached for a glass of San Miguel.

"What do you mean?" he asked.

Lin said, "James went to Vienna to safeguard something called the Spear of Destiny. Do you know what that is?"

Zanir nodded his head. "I know, I know what it is."

"The Chinese are trying to steal the spear," she said. "James is there to stop it."

Zanir took another sip of beer.

"We never knew about that part," said Zanir. "This is the first I'm hearing about it. What else do you know?" asked Zanir.

"That's it," said Lin. "That's all James told me."

"The Chinese want Die Glocke too, that's why we're here. But there's something else," said Zanir.

"What do you mean?" asked Lin.

Zanir looked into Lin's eyes.

"Sounds like the Chinese have a three part plan: Get the Spear of Destiny, get Die Glocke, and kill James Ross."

A look of shock spread across Lin's face.

"What?" Lin said.

"That's right," said Zanir. "The Chinese are here to kill James. They have a vendetta against him for the killing of Admiral Shui Gui last week in the Bahamas."

"But," said Lin, "James didn't kill Shui Gui. Emanuel did."

Zanir shook his head.

"It doesn't really much matter. They think he did and that's what they believe," said Zanir.

*I've got to warn James,* thought Lin.

One of the men at the Chinese table nonchalantly leaned down and rolled a small object towards the middle of the room.

*BANG!*

A blinding flash followed the loud explosion as a stun grenade ignited.

The dining room went into full panic mode. Tables and chairs were overturned with food and drinks flying helter-skelter as couples screamed and ran for the exit with smoke filling the once tranquil scene. The smoke set off the overhead sprinkler system.

Zanir kicked over their table as he, Shiloah, and Lin took cover behind it. The Mossad men pulled out their Jericho 941 pistols. The Chinese men had already disappeared.

"They've gone to the garage!" yelled Zanir above the chaos.

"Come on!" Lin yelled. "Through the kitchen!"

Lin sprang up and raced towards the kitchen with the Mossad men closely following. The kitchen was in a state of utter confusion as Lin and the Mossad men ran through it at the same time that the kitchen staff was running towards the dining room to see what happened.

Lin flung open the rear exit door and led the Mossad men through when the darkness of the night was quickly shattered by bright flashes of what looked like angry wasps spinning back and forth.

*KA-POW!*

*KA-POW!*

*KA-POW!*

A pitched gunfight in front of the garage had started between Yatom, Harel, and the Chinese agents.

Zanir and Shiloah joined the fight.

*KA-POW!*

*KA-POW!*

*KA-POW!*

Lin hunched down and circled behind the Mossad men. She sprinted to the left side of the garage and went in through the side door. Flicking on the bank of overhead florescent lights, Lin stood in awe of the mechanism known as Die Glocke.

*Get moving girl.*

Lin grabbed a hold of the circular submarine-type hatch handle and frantically spun it counterclockwise. It opened with a bone-chilling high-pitched screech. She ducked her head and jumped inside the hatch and sat in the Luftwaffe pilot seat.

*I've watched James do this several times,* she thought.

Lin checked to make sure the SS dagger was still firmly in the engagement slot. The original gangschaltung gearshift lever had broken off in Ross's hands a while ago. She saw the instruction sheet still on the instrument panel where Ross had left it. There were seven steps she needed to go through to use Die Glocke.

Bullets from the gun battle outside were now zipping through the front garage doors.

*I've got to get out of here NOW!*

Realizing she needed to combine steps, Lin reached forward and flipped up the plastic safety cover on the macht auf (on/off) switch and pressed the button, which immediately started to glow an ancient amber luminescence. She reached forward and secured the front hatch. Knowing there wasn't any time to preset the trip parameters, she ran her fingers haphazardly across Die Glocke's mechanical sprocket calendar date-time dial. The dial was divided into two parts: where you were and where you were going.

*None of that matters now, I've just got to get out of here!*

Then she ratcheted the dagger backwards.

*Clack, clack, clack.*

The sounds coincided with the spinning of the control panel's mechanical sprocket calendar dial.

*Clack, clack, clack.*

If Lin could have seen the outside of Die Glocke, she would have been amazed. The base of the machine was emitting a greenish-orange glow, and the entire outer capsule was starting to vibrate. The clacking sound inside was in competition with a swirling, rushing, windstorm sound outside growing in intensity. Inside Die Glocke, her body was immediately flushed with an overpowering sense of peaceful bliss. She thought she might pass out.

*Got to fight it. Got to buckle myself in.*

Lin groped for the fallschirmjäger harness and buckled herself into the contoured Luftwaffe pilot seat.

*KA-BOOM!*

The twin barn-type front garage doors disappeared in a blast of splintered wood and metal. But it was too late.

The Chinese and Israeli agents watched in amazement as Die Glocke became an enormous greenish-orange glowing orb while whirling and humming in front of them.

"Don't shoot at it! Don't destroy it!" yelled the Chinese team leader to his men.

Then Die Glocke simply vanished amidst a whirlwind of swirling dust and crackling static electricity.

*KA-POW!*

*KA-POW!*

*KA-POW!*

Two of the Chinese fell in a hail of Mossad gunfire. Seeing this, the third member of the Chinese team turned and ran off into the darkness of the night.

"Let him go," said Zanir waving off his three colleagues.

The four Mossad men walked into the garage.

They stood in front of the spot where Die Glocke had been just seconds earlier.

There they stared down at the concrete floor and saw a sizzling, steaming, crystallized sheet of glass.

Zanir crouched down looking at it and said, "Oh my God."

# *PART THREE*

*Whatever happens to you has been waiting to happen since the beginning of time.*

Marcus Aurelius Antoninus
121 — 180 AD
Roman Emperor

# *CHAPTER FOURTEEN*

# *TIME RIDER*

Die Glocke was hurtling through time and space — backwards. It was traveling into the past. Lin looked at the instrument panel and saw that she was now passing through 1881.

*Got to correct this,* she thought to herself.

Lin reached for the SS dagger, which now acted as the control lever, and slowly pushed it forward. Die Glocke's mechanical sprocket calendar date-time dial started to reverse course and shifted the trajectory into the future. Then she flipped up the plastic safety cover of the vintage global positioning system and pushed the latitude-longitude button. A world map displayed on the 1940s-era screen, and she searched for Austria.

*Okay, let's see,* thought Lin as she scanned the map.

*There it is.*

Lin punched in the latitude and longitude for Vienna Austria. Then the world map closed to materialize as an Austrian map. She found

Vienna and tapped in those coordinates. The screen map changed yet again to a Vienna City map this time.

"This is probably a 1944 map," said Lin talking to herself.

"Let's see ..."

She located the Hofburg Palace and found a large forested area behind it. On either side of the forest appeared to be what looked like vast open fields.

Lin inputed the eight digit grid coordinates for the closest open field to the palace. Then she looked back at the calendar dial and set it to today's date.

*This has got to work,* she thought. *James and I share the same destiny. I know we do.*

While carefully counting the dates, Lin gently pushed the dagger to the *STOP* position.

*I'm here,* thought Lin.

The blissful feeling Lin had experienced was suddenly replaced with a dull, throbbing headache. It felt like seasickness.

*Oh God,* thought Lin as she grabbed her queasy stomach.

Die Glocke had miraculously come to rest on a grassy spot directly between several trees, and not more than two kilometers from the Hofburg museum.

Lin pulled the SS dagger out of its gear slot and slid it behind her belt. Without that make-shift control lever, no one could use Die Glocke for time travel purposes. Then she saw Ross's red wool jacket lying next to the pilot's seat and put it on. She reached forward and spun the circular handle on the exit counterclockwise. The hatch opened to reveal a snow frosted field. Lin lowered her head and stepped up and over through the open hatch. Once outside she turned around and slammed shut the hatch and spun the handle clockwise. Then she vomited on the snow.

Lin reached down and grabbed a handful of snow. She rubbed some across her face and crunched some in her mouth.

*Got to call James,* she thought.

Lin reached inside her bluejeans pocket and pulled out her iPhone. She scrolled through her contacts until she found Ross.

*Bzzz.*

*Bzzz.*

*Bzzz.*

Ross looked at his Samsung and answered.

"Lin?" said Ross.

"Oh Jamie, thank God," replied Lin breathlessly. "I'm here!"

"In Vienna?" asked Ross incredulously.

"Yes, and Lailani's place was attacked by Chinese agents looking for the Bell," said Lin out of breath.

"Where are you exactly?" asked Ross.

Lin looked around the frozen field. Her breath was coming out in huffs and puffs circling skyward and then disappearing.

"I'm in a field about two kilometers northeast of the museum. Behind me is a forested area, and in front of me I see a huge Mozart monument."

"Did you drive here or …"

"No. I took the Bell. They were after it," gasped Lin.

"Okay, okay." Ross thought for a second. "Activate the GPS tracker on your phone, and I'll use mine to find you. I'll be there just as soon as I can. Just wait for me okay?"

"Okay my love," replied Lin.

"Right, see you soon," said Ross and then he hung up.

Lon Inus looked at Ross across the table in the coffee shop.

"Trouble?" asked Inus.

Ross put his Samsung in his pocket.

"A complication," said Ross. "My girlfriend is here and I need to go pick her up," explained Ross.

"Miss Sparrow? Here in Vienna?" asked Inus.

*How does he know Lin Sparrow is my girlfriend?* thought Ross.

Ross assumed Emanuel must have told Inus all about him and Lin.

"Yeah, there was an attack on the restaurant owned by Emanuel's cousins."

Inus sat up.

"What happened?" he asked.

Ross said, "Lin just told me a Chinese team attacked it. She didn't wait around for the outcome."

Inus became deadly serious.

"When did this happen?" he asked.

"Evidently just now," said Ross.

"Then there's no time to lose," said Inus standing up. He reached in his pocket and threw thirty Euros on the table. "Let's go."

Ross and Inus left the coffee shop and hurried over to Mariahilfer Strasse.

"This is my car," said Inus, as he pointed to the Audi A5 Cabriolet.

Inus clicked his auto remote twice and said, "Get in."

Ross opened the passenger door of the black car and sat down.

"Here," said Inus as he pressed the ignition button and the turbocharged 3.0 liter V6 engine roared to life. "Put Lin's location in the GPS."

Ross plugged his Samsung into the GPS and inputted Lin's cellphone number. In a few seconds an exact location appeared on the dashboard screen.

"Here she is," said Ross staring at the screen.

Inus performed a flawless racing change into fifth gear and passed a beige Volvo.

"That looks like the Burggarten," said Inus.

Ross asked, "What's that?"

"It's a park now, but it was a Napoleonic battlefield in the early 1800s. I know how to get there."

Inus downshifted and turned onto Ringstrassen Boulevard. He could tell what Ross was thinking.

"Do not worry my friend. The park is full of statues and monuments. There's even a Mozart statue which has a whole labyrinth of tunnels beneath it. Perhaps passersby will simply think Die Glocke is just another exhibit."

"You know about Die Glocke, the Bell?" asked Ross.

Inus pressed the clutch and shifted again.

"Yes."

Thinking quickly, Inus said, "Emanuel told me."

*Actually I've known about Die Glocke long before you were even born my young friend,* thought Inus.

Inus mechanically shifted gears again.

*I've known about Die Glocke since it was but an idea in the mind of Obergruppenführer Hans Friedrich Kammler's head.*

Large flakes of wet snow were coming down more plentiful as the black Audi A5 Cabriolet made its way towards the park. Inus flicked on the windshield wipers.

"When this is all over I've vowed to destroy Die Glocke," said Ross looking at Inus.

"Good idea," said Inus. "Perhaps the world is not ready for Die Glocke. Can you imagine what could happen if the Chinese got a hold of it? They could travel to the future and install a compromised man as President of the United States, someone that they totally corrupted and controlled. Because how goes America soon goes the rest of the world. Once America falls into the Chinese orbit, the rest of the countries of the world would fall into place. They would soon realize resistance would be futile. The world would be enslaved by communist thugs."

"Yeah it could turn out real bad," said Ross.

Inus nodded his head.

"The past is the past. We can't change it," said Inus.

Ross stared out his window.

"But what if we could change the past, for the good? What if we could correct a mistake?" asked Ross.

"It would have to be carefully regulated," said Inus. "And my reading of mankind over the years tells me it would never work."

Ross looked at Inus.

"No matter how hard we try," replied Inus.

"But," said Inus, "there are always exceptions to everything."

Inus knew Ross had used Die Glocke to rescue Lin. He gave Ross what he wanted to hear.

"Only for love is the past worth changing."

"There's the park," said Ross pointing with his finger.

Inus slowed the Audi down and they coasted into Burggarten Park.

"Give me some specific directions," said Inus.

Ross enlarged the GPS screen image with his fingers.

"Looks like she is up here to the left, right around this little row of trees," said Ross.

Ross phoned Lin on his Samsung.

"Lin, we're here. We're in a black Audi. Can you see us?" said Ross.

"Tell her we're beeping our horn twice," said Inus, and then he sounded the Cabriolet's horn.

Lin heard the horn and ran from behind the snow covered trees.

"Yes I see you now," said Lin. "I'm coming." She turned and looked back at Die Glocke which was already beginning to get covered by fresh snow.

Ross had already sprung from the car and was running towards Lin. Inus put the Audi in park and watched as Ross and Lin embraced in the middle of the frosted field.

*They are in love,* thought Inus. *Surely they are in love.*

Lin reached out and locked her arms around his neck, pulling Ross close in a timeless embrace.

Their lips met in a sweetly reassuring kiss.

The warmth of the kiss lingered, giving her the proof she needed that this was indeed real and happening now.

Lin pulled back and looked into Ross's eyes.

His eyes glistened with tears, and his lips curled up in a little smile.

Lin reached out and brushed away a tear from his cheek.

"I love you James," she said.

"I love you too," said Ross.

Ross allowed his nostrils to fill with Lin's luxurious scent. It intoxicated him, and for a second he was swirling through time and space.

There was no present, no past; no danger, no enemy; no regret, no despair.

There was only the kiss.

But then the moment was over, and he reached up and took Lin's arms from around his neck.

"Come on," said Ross.

Hand-in-hand Ross led Lin through the snow field to the Audi.

"I've got someone helping me here," said Ross. "He's a friend of Emanuel."

"A friend of Emanuel?" said Lin.

"Yeah. His name is Lon Inus. He's waiting for us in the car."

"But how? How did that happen?" asked Lin.

Ross tried to explain quickly.

"Emanuel had a CD in his car addressed to me, so I played it on the way over and it talked about this guy. Emanuel knew my entire mission somehow."

"I guess that doesn't really surprise me, knowing Emanuel," said Lin.

Inus was outside of the Audi holding open a door for them.

"Lin," said Ross quickly, "this is my friend Lon Inus."

Lin and Inus shook hands.

"Pleased to meet you Lin," said Inus.

Ross sat in the back and Lin took the passenger seat next to Inus.

"Let's get outta here," said Ross.

Inus put the Audi in gear and discreetly drove through Burggarten Park. He glanced over at Lin. She looked cold and tired.

"I think I better take you straight back to your hotel," said Inus.

# *CHAPTER FIFTEEN*

# *SWITCH*

The four-member People's Archeology Team was inside the Hofburg restoration workshop. They had their replica of the Longinus Spear and were comparing it to the original under prearranged direct supervision by two members of the Hofburg restoration staff, Johann and Wernher.

Nü Jiangshi and her executive officer Ming Chen were getting ready to enact their carefully planned ruse to switch the spears.

Wutu Shen had the replica spear in his left hand, and was checking the heft of it compared to the real spear in his right hand. He was in the process of placing down both spears on the workshop table when suddenly he moaned.

"I don't feel so good …"

Then he gasped for breath, groaned and hunched over, spinning around with both spears clutched to his chest, and collapsed to the floor.

"Wutu!" cried out Nü Jiangshi.

"Help him someone!" yelled Ming Chen.

Utter confusion enveloped the restoration workshop.

Johann and Wernher looked at each other.

"Call emergency services!" directed Johann to Wernher.

Wernher ran to the door and pulled down the red handle on the emergency services alarm.

*BRANG!*

*BRANG!*

*BRANG!*

Ming Chen knelt over Wutu and started loosening his clothes and treating him for shock. Chong Zee grabbed the spears and slid them across the floor away from Wutu.

"Oh my God help him," cried Chong.

"Where are the paramedics?" demanded Ming.

"Does anyone know CPR?" said Nü.

Fearing the worst, Johann and Wernher knelt down on either side of Wutu and tried to assist however they could.

In this confusion and chaos, Nü was able to walk over and pick up the spears, clutching them to her bosom.

*These are as identical as can be,* thought Nü to herself.

Then Nü placed one on the table and the other in the People's Archeology Team travel bag. The replica had a small piece of tape on the blade designating it as the copy. Nü was careful to surreptitiously switch the tape before she placed that spear on the table.

*They will never have the nerve to search our bag,* thought Nü. *They won't want to cause an international incident with the People's Republic of China.*

Nü smirked sardonically.

*They are too afraid of us.*

Then the door banged open and the paramedic team rushed in.

"Make way, make way now please," said the team leader.

The crowd around Wutu evaporated as the paramedics moved in and took over. An oxygen mask was applied to his face and an intravenous line was started.

"You're going to be all right sir," said a paramedic.

A stretcher was expanded and the medics placed Wutu on it.

"We'll take him to the clinic for observation."

Johann looked relieved and said, "Thank you."

Wernher was sweating profusely over the excitement and mopped his brow with his handkerchief.

"We're so very sorry this happened," said Wernher.

Nü had forced herself to tear up.

"I just hope Wutu will be all right, he's so fragile," said Nü feinting sympathy.

"Oh yes, quite, quite," said Johann. "Mister Wutu will be fine, fine. He's in very good hands."

"Yes of course," chimed in Wernher. "Our medical facilities are the best there are. And he'll be well taken care of, I assure you."

Nü had to control the conversation now, and the situation. She knew she had to divert attention away from the spear inspection and get her team out of there as quickly and efficiently as she could, with the real spear.

"Perhaps, if you don't mind, we can delay the inspection for a day or two," asked Nü with tears in her eyes.

"Yes," chimed in Ming. "I think I'm feeling faint myself."

Wernher looked alarmingly at Johann.

"Oh my, of course, of course, you must all return to your hotel and get some rest. Try not to worry. We'll keep you informed of the status of Mister Wutu. Just try to relax tonight," said Wernher.

"Certainly," said Johann. "I'm going to have a car take you all back to your hotel now. Don't worry about a thing. And of course this is the right thing to do. We all understand. And please don't worry. I assure you Mister Wutu will be well taken care of. Just try to relax tonight."

Nü wiped away her tears.

"Perhaps you're right. We all need a break today. Thank you, thank you so much sincerely."

Johann and Wernher bowed to Nü.

Nü returned the bow.

*I've got them now,* thought Nü. *They're so afraid of offending they won't dare question anything we do.*

Nü picked up the bag containing the real Longinus Spear.

Johann held open the door and Wernher escorted the team out of the Hofburg.

*What a mess,* thought Johann.

He walked over and picked up the spear on the table. Then he placed the spear on a red silk cloth and wrapped it around it.

*Got to return this to the display case right now before anything else happens!*

Wernher led the Chinese team to the waiting van out front.

"Please don't worry," said Wernher again as he held open the door of the van. "Everything will be all right, and we will keep you informed of Mister Wutu's status."

Nü took a hold of both of Wernher's hands and bowed her head.

"Thank you for all of your kindness today," she said.

"You are entirely welcome," replied Wernher. Then he stuck his head in the van and said to the driver, "Please take them back to the Park Hyatt Hotel on Innere Stadt. Thank you."

Wernher slid the van door shut and waved.

Inside the van the three remaining members of the team all looked at each other.

Nü clutched the bag containing the authentic Spear of Destiny.

*Success.*

# *CHAPTER SIXTEEN*

# *SECOND STRIKE*

Inus pulled his black Audi A5 Cabriolet to the valet station of the Herrenhof Steigenberger Hotel. The three friends exited the car and Inus dropped off the keys with the attendant.

Walking up the steps into the hotel, Inus turned to Ross and said, "I've got a bad feeling something has happened to the spear. We need to deal with the Chinese team today. I'll wait for you in the lounge."

"Okay," said Ross. "Let me get Lin settled in first."

They silently rode the elevator up to the third floor.

Ross led Lin to room 323 and held the door open for her.

No sooner had Ross turned to close the door than Lin was violently grabbed by the forearm and tossed across the bed.

"James!" she screamed.

Ross turned around to see the flash of a suppressed pistol firing at him.

*Pffft!*

*Pffft!*

The bullets splintered into the doorframe next to Ross's head.

With no time to think but only react, Ross lunged across the room and jumped on his attacker. He grabbed the man's gun hand and knocked the pistol to the carpet. In an instant Ross recognized the handgun as a Weisheng Shou Qiang (QSW-06) suppressed semiautomatic in 5.8x21mm caliber.

*Chinese Special Forces,* thought Ross.

Ross and the Chinese assassin struggled for a second, then Ross lifted the man up, twisting, and body slammed him to the floor with Ross on top of him.

*The American is an animal!* thought the Chinese assassin.

A master of Wing Chun martial art, like lightning the assassin struck Ross in his solar plexus and pummeled Ross with a series of closed-fist blows to his chest. Ross blocked several of the strikes and then threw a smashing right fist to the assassin's jaw. The man's head violently snapped back.

Lin snatched up the suppressed pistol and aimed it at the assassin. But Ross already had both hands around the man's neck. The assassin squirmed under Ross's weight and flailed away at him, punching and clawing wildly, while gasping for breath.

*Die bastard die,* thought Ross as he pressed and squeezed the assassin's neck.

And then the assassin's mouth was open with his tongue protruding hideously, and his eyes rolled back. Ross relaxed his grip and leaned back, but just to be sure the man was dead, Ross slammed the palm of his right hand across the man's chin until it bent his neck with a sickening *crack.*

Ross leaned back on his haunches and wobbly stood up.

"Are you okay Lin?" he asked.

"Yes," said Lin as she handed the gun to Ross.

Ross hefted the pistol in his hand.

"This is a pistol used by Chinese Special Forces," said Ross. "Let's see who this guy is."

Ross leaned over the man and reached into his jacket. He pulled out a Hofburg Museum Distinguished Visitor Pass.

"Mister Chong Zee," read Ross off the document. "Member of the People's Republic of China Archeology Team."

Lin said, "It was a Chinese team that attacked the restaurant in Zurich too."

Ross rolled the body over. He searched him and pulled out a wallet.

"Let's see what we have here," said Ross flipping through the wallet. "Chinese drivers license, Communist Party ID, pocket archeology credentials, money."

"But why, why attack us in Zurich and now here in the hotel? It doesn't make sense," said Lin.

Ross replied, "It makes sense if you realize that Xi Jinping wants to dominate the world and shows strength in every move he makes. He is very methodical and plans everything. He is not afraid to demonstrate force, and he actively relies on the West to be afraid of conflict and not want to ruffle his feathers."

Lin said, "So Xi must really believe in the power of the spear to have no fear of killing anyone standing in his way."

Ross nodded.

"Xi was given a wide berth when the Democrats occupied the White House. Democrat administrations have notoriously bowed down to China, but not without getting millions of dollars for their complacency. They call that *influence peddling.* I call it selling out your country. The Democrat administrations took millions from China, basically in bribes, for the assurance that our corrupt politicians would shift national policy to favor China. Look at how we shifted to electric vehicles and stopped drilling for oil. Well, the United States was the world's leading producer of oil and natural gas under President Trump. But when the Democrats took over they came up with the phony climate crisis hoax and stopped drilling to go electric instead. Who do you think owned the lithium that was used to produce the very expensive batteries used for electric vehicles? China. China has the market on lithium. And China also took over the lithium in Afghanistan after our disastrous withdrawal of forces perpetrated by the last Democrat administration."

Lin said, "I'll never understand American politics."

Ross replied, "Neither do I. China has many proxies. For instance, Iran could do nothing until China gives them the go-ahead. Then Iran would give Hamas and Hezbollah the funding and the okay to attack Israel. That's the way it works. We used to say Iran was the number one financier of terrorism in the world, while all the time Iran would do nothing without the okay from China."

"China wants to rule the world," said Lin.

Ross nodded his head.

"And if they get the Longinus Spear in their hands they have a good shot," replied Ross.

Then Ross took Lin by the hand and sat on the bed.

"Here look at this" said Ross.

He unfolded the napkin he had written on and showed Lin the names.

LON G. INUS

LONGINUS

Lin stared incredulously at the crinkled napkin.

"Longinus?" she asked, taking the napkin in her hands.

"Yeah," sighed Ross.

"You mean you think this guy is actually *the* Longinus? The Longinus who pierced the side of Christ with the spear, thousands of years ago?"

"I don't know Lin, but he seems to know all about the Chinese team that's here. He knows who they are, their names. He knows where they're staying."

Lin sat down on the bed staring at the napkin.

"He knows everything about the spear," said Ross. "He knows about past attempts to steal the spear. He knows its history. And he was friends with Emanuel."

"Emanuel," said Lin. "You know what that means? With Emanuel, all things were possible. I mean, we both saw him disappear right out of the cockpit of that plane."

"I know," said Ross. "I know."

Lin looked at the corpse of the Chinese assassin on the floor.

"What are we going to do about this body?"

Ross picked up the receiver of the room courtesy phone and pressed the button for the front desk.

"Hello? This is James Ross in room 323. Can you please page Mister Lon Inus for me? He's in the lounge downstairs. Yes that's right. Lon Inus. Please ask him to come up to my room. Yes. Right away. Thank you."

Inus received the page and hurried to room 323. Ross let him inside and showed him the body.

"This guy was waiting for us inside the room. Somehow he got in. He attacked us. He's a member of the Chinese Archeology Team," said Ross.

Inus knelt down and turned the corpse's head back and forth.

"Yeah he's dead all right. Broken neck," said Inus.

Inus stood up and looked at Ross and Lin.

"Are you two all right?"

Lin nodded her head and Ross said, "Yeah we're fine."

"We've got to get rid of this body," said Ross.

Inus thought for a second.

"Is there a mens room on this floor?" asked Inus.

"Yeah, just down the hall," replied Ross.

"I think we should carry this man down the hall as if he were intoxicated, and take him into the mens room, set him in a stall, and leave," said Inus.

Ross looked at Lin. She nodded approval.

"Okay let's do it," said Ross.

Ross knelt down and searched the assassin one more time. He removed his wallet, cellphone, museum pass, and pocketed them.

"We may need these," said Ross.

Then Ross and Inus picked up the body of Chong Zee. Each man hooked their arm under Chong's and basically dragged him upright. Lin hurried over and opened the door.

"The bathrooms are to the left," said Lin.

Inus and Ross carried Chong Zee's body about seventy-five feet down the hall to the mens room. Ross kicked open the door with his foot .

Inside was a man in his middle thirties who was just finishing washing his hands.

"I'm afraid our friend has had a little too much to drink," said Inus smiling and looking at the man at the sink.

The man smiled and dried his hands quickly.

"I know the feeling," he said smiling and then exited the mens room.

Ross and Inus opened a stall and placed the corpse on the toilet. Then they locked the stall door and washed their hands.

"Let's get outta here," said Ross.

"Right," replied Inus.

They both left the mens room and walked back to room 323.

Once inside the room, Inus said, "Do you have any weapons with you?"

"Yeah," said Ross, "we've got this," and he handed Inus the assassin's suppressed pistol. Then he went over to the room safe and opened it. "And I've got this Beretta."

Inus looked at the Chinese pistol in his hand, and the Beretta that Ross was holding.

"Great," replied Inus. "These will come in handy."

In her room at the Park Hyatt Vienna Hotel, Nü Jiangshi phoned her colleague Chong Zee, but got no answer.

"Something's not right," said Nü. "He would answer. And he should have been back thirty minutes ago."

Chong Zee was dead, and Wutu Shen was still being treated at the medical clinic. That left only Ming Chen and Nü. In a little less than two hours, the People's Republic of China Ministry of State Security Team had been cut in half. Then Nü's phone rang.

Bzzz.

Bzzz.

Bzzz.

Nü answered the phone, speaking in Mandarin.

"Yes. Yes. Un-huh. Mm. Seriously? When did this happen? Really. Okay, okay. Yes I understand. I will take care of it. Yes thank you. Goodbye."

"What was that?" asked Ming.

"That was Colonel Weng. It seems our team in Zurich has been decimated. Complete mission failure," said Nü.

"What?" said Ming.

"Yes. The attempt to get Die Glocke was met with fierce resistance in Zurich. Evidently members of Israeli Mossad were involved, and Miss Lin Sparrow too."

"And what about the machine?" asked Ming.

Nü paced back and forth in the room.

"It's disappeared, gone, vanished."

Ming looked worried. She knew failure meant only death awaited them if they made it back to China.

"Do not worry," said Nü. "We've got the spear, and Zurich was not our mission. But I swear to you that I will kill this damn American soldier and his bitch of a girlfriend."

"And I will help you," said Ming standing up proudly.

Nü looked at Ming and caressed her cheek.

"Yes you will," said Nü. Then Nü leaned in and kissed Ming full on the open mouth. Ming returned the kiss and their tongues explored each other sensuously.

Nü pulled back and walked over to the room courtesy safe and opened it. She took out the Spear of Destiny.

Hefting the spear in her hand, Nü said, "Call Wutu at the clinic. Tell him he's just had a miraculous recovery and to get over here right away. Tell him to bring his equipment."

Then Nü said, "Before this day is done, I swear to you I will stab this spear into the heart of Captain James Ross."

Nü took Ming by the hand and walked into the bedroom. She dropped the spear to the floor and pushed Ming onto the bed. Then she closed the door.

# *CHAPTER SEVENTEEN*

# *DEAL*

Ross and Inus were sitting down and enjoying a cup of coffee in the room while Lin took the opportunity to take a quick shower.

"The Chinese have the spear in their hotel," said Inus. "And they must realize that their colleague is not coming back, so they may attempt to flee to the airport."

"Possibly," replied Ross, "but what can you tell me about the team leader, this woman Nü Jiangshi?"

Inus took a sip and then placed his cup back down on the saucer.

"She's a fanatic," said Inus. "Nü Jiangshi is totally dedicated to textbook communism. She would sell out her own mother for advancement."

Ross thought for a second.

"So they've got the spear, probably in their hotel room, and are set to fly out of Vienna the day after tomorrow?" said Ross.

"That's right," replied Inus.

Ross looked at his Benrus. Its blade-type hands told him it was 1932 hours. He stood up and started pacing back and forth.

"What if I just called her?" said Ross.

The question caught Inus midstream in sipping his coffee and he choked a little.

"What?" asked Inus.

Ross said, "What if I just called Miss Nü Jiangshi and offered her something more valuable than the spear?"

Lin walked out of the bathroom in a white hotel robe and was toweling dry her hair.

"You mean like a time machine? Like Die Glocke?" answered Lin.

"Exactly," said Ross.

Inus snapped his fingers. "I think I understand," said Inus. "You mean to lure them away from the hotel with the spear, to possibly trade for Die Glocke?"

"Yeah," said Ross. "Getting possession of Die Glocke would be a coup for Miss Jiangshi. And if her superiors found out they had left Die Glocke here without attempting to recover it …"

"That could just be the difference between getting promoted and getting shot when they went home," said Inus.

Lin sat down and poured herself a cup of coffee.

"Do you know that the word *Jiangshi* in Cantonese means walking corpse, or actually reanimated corpse. Basically it means vampire," said Lin.

"How do you know that Lin?" asked Inus.

Lin said, "Because there's a whole genre of jiangshi films in East Asia. I used to watch them when I was growing up in Malaysia. There's books too."

Ross stop pacing and sat down.

"So, I'll call Miss Vampire on her colleagues phone, and ask her to swap. We'll have them follow us to where you left Die Glocke," said Ross nodding to Lin, "and we'll ambush them and get the spear."

Inus leaned forward in his chair and put down his coffee cup.

"It could work," he said. "It could work."

"Okay," said Ross. "Then that's the plan."

Lin stood up.

"I'll change quick and be right with you," she said. Then Lin walked into the bathroom.

When the bathroom door was closed, Ross pulled his chair closer to Inus and said, "Lin knows how to operate Die Glocke. Let's agree that she should be inside it in case anything goes wrong, so she can escape."

Inus looked into Ross's eyes.

"Agreed," said Inus.

Inus thought, *So it comes down to Burggarten. The park that was a battlefield. It became the castle garden of the Hofburg in 1819, sitting on top of the ruins of the Augustinerschanze fortifications from the Battle of Wagram that took place there from 4 to 6 July 1809. It was Emperor Napoleon's French Army against the Austrian Army of Archduke Charles. Wagram was the largest battle in European history up to that time. Napoleon initially won by defeating the Austrian forces and occupying Vienna in early May of 1809, but he was later defeated at the Battle of Aspern-Essling. It took Napoleon six weeks and 172,000 men to counterattack on July the 4th in what is now called the Battle of Wagram. Napoleon completed a successful river crossing of the Danube with his forces and launched a series of attacks. On July the 6th Archduke Charles admitted defeat. Blood from the bodies of 74,000 soldiers stain that hallowed ground. And this will be the next battlefront between good and evil; between freedom and tyranny; between Christ and Satan.*

Lin came out of the bathroom dressed in bluejeans, sneakers, a blue sweater, and wearing Ross's red wool jacket. Ross was wearing his traditional black suit, white cotton shirt, narrow black necktie, and black shoes. Inus was still in his black suit.

Ross picked up the dead assassin's phone and scrolled to the most recent phone call. He figured that would have been Nü Jiangshi calling him.

"Okay here we go," said Ross. He put the phone on *speaker* and pushed the *recall* button.

Bzzz.

Bzzz.

Bzzz.

"Hāi," answered a female voice on the other end of the phone.

Ross was taking a chance guessing that it would be Nü Jiangshi answering the phone.

"Hello, this is James Ross. Who is this please?"

Nü was shocked.

*What boldness,* she thought. *What absolute audacity.*

"Yes, hello," said Nü. "I thought this was my friend's phone. Could you please put him on for me?"

"Um, Mister Chong Zee can't come to the phone right now," said Ross.

"Oh," said Nü. "I understand. How can I help you then?"

"Listen," said Ross, "I'm calling you to make a deal. I know you have the Spear of Destiny, otherwise you would not have sent Mister Zee to greet us."

"I'm afraid I don't understand what you are talking about Mister Ross," said Nü.

"Look, I know who you are," said Ross. "Miss Nü Jiangshi."

"Yes," said Nü. "That is my name."

"And I know who you work for," said Ross.

There was a moment of silence on the other end.

"I am the team leader of the People's Republic of China Archeology Team," replied Nü.

"Yeah," said Ross, "and you also work for the Ministry of State Security."

Nü held her hand over the receiver and looked at Ming.

Ming nodded her head.

Nü went back to the phone call.

"I'm listening," said Nü.

"I'd like to make a deal with you," said Ross.

"What kind of deal?" asked Nü.

"I'll give you Die Glocke for the spear," answered Ross.

There was silence on the other end.

"Did you hear me? I said I'll give you Die Glocke for the Spear of Destiny," repeated Ross.

"Why should I agree to this?" said Nü. "I have the spear and I'll get Die Glocke anyway."

Ross looked at Lin and Inus.

"You'll never get Die Glocke because I'm the only one who knows where it is."

More silence on Nü's phone.

"Did you hear me?" asked Ross impatiently.

"Yes," said Nü. "All right. When and where?"

Ross gave the thumbs up to Inus.

"Tonight. One hour from now. I'll text you directions where to meet me."

"All right James," said Nü. "You know, I have actually seen you before. Do you remember? At the Spear of Destiny exhibit this morning. We had a moment."

Ross thought back for a second.

"Yes I remember you," said Ross.

"I'll be anxiously waiting for your text, James," said Nü.

Then she hung up the phone.

Inus said, "We've got to plan this perfectly. If they ambush us, we lose the spear and Die Glocke."

"What do you suggest?" said Ross

Inus looked at Lin.

"Lin here knows how to operate Die Glocke. Let's get her over there quickly and inside the machine," said Inus. "If there is treachery she can activate the machine and get out of there. And I'm the only one who can verify if the spear is real or not, so I need to be up front with you to greet Miss Vampire."

Ross thought for a second.

"Okay, then it will have to be the Burggarten parking lot we were in today," said Ross. "I'll text them the location of the parking lot."

He hated getting Lin involved at all, but he had to admit that Inus was right. If the plan fell apart, Lin could activate Die Glocke and disappear with it.

Inus pulled the magazine out of the Chinese QSW-06 pistol.

"Did you know this thing takes a twenty round magazine?" said Inus. "It's got eighteen bullets left. How about you?"

Ross said, "My Beretta takes eight in the mag, and I've got two more extra mags."

Ross put the Beretta 71 in his right side suit coat pocket, and the two spare magazines in his left.

Inus unscrewed the suppressor and put it in his suit coat pocket. He slid the pistol behind the front waistband of his pants and belt, and then buttoned up his suit coat.

"Ready?" asked Inus.

Frustrated, Lin asked, "You really think you can trust the Chinese to follow through with this? What if they attack us leaving the hotel, or simply leaving the room?"

Inus looked at Ross and Lin with sad eyes.

*What a fool I am,* thought Inus. *These young people are in love, like I was once. The thought of either one losing the other is overwhelming. I should just do this myself.*

"Maybe you would like some time alone?" asked Inus.

He looked at his 1940 Eterna chronograph wristwatch.

"I'll be out front in the car, waiting."

Then Inus left the room.

Ross looked at Lin and took her hand. He gave her a reassuring smile.

"Lin, it's the only way," said Ross. "Inus is right. Only he can identify the real Longinus Spear …"

"Because he *is* Longinus," said Lin.

Ross sat down in a chair.

"You really think so?" he said.

Lin pulled a chair beside Ross and sat down.

"I know so," she said. "I could feel it the moment we met. The way he talked, the way he carried himself, his knowledge of esoteric things. He's Longinus all right. I mean, look at his name — Lon G. Inus?"

"I know," said Ross.

"And don't forget he's friends with Emanuel. And how did Emanuel know to give you that CD, and in his car? How did he even know you would be driving his car? That CD described exactly what is happening to us now, and what we have to do."

"Yeah …"

"And Longinus was waiting for you at lunch? And he so easily threw in with you? And the way he looks?"

"What do you mean?" asked Ross

"I mean the mediterranean face, the hair, the eyes. I mean, it's not too hard to picture him in a Roman tunic."

"Yeah," said Ross. "But he's our friend now, just like Emanuel was, and whether it was all part of some grand majestic plan, destiny, or just plain happenstance, we need him."

"I know, I know," said Lin. "The Spear of Destiny is important. We can't let it fall into communist hands. We have to safeguard it and return it to the Hofburg."

"And," said Ross, "Longinus is our best bet to do that."

Lin smiled at her boyfriend, the completely wonderfully charming man she had met just a short time ago, and with whom she had shared so many dangerous adventures already.

"So what happened to just turning them over to INTERPOL?" she asked teasingly.

Ross smiled and a comma of his brown hair fell across his forehead.

Lin reached over and brushed it up. Looking into his eyes, she placed her hand behind Ross's neck and pulled him close. Their lips met in a warm gentle kiss.

Ross wished the moment could last forever. He wished time could suddenly just stand still. But then reality hit him and he stood up.

"Let's go," said Ross.

They left the room holding hands and walked down the hall past the mens room, taking notice that there was absolutely no activity there. The couple then rode the elevator down to the lobby, each alone in their individual thoughts.

# *CHAPTER EIGHTEEN*

# *THIRD STRIKE*

Ross and Lin walked to the entrance of the Herrenhof Steigenberger Hotel. The heavy glass entrance doors automatically hissed open for them. They stepped out into the night and were greeted by soft wintry snowflakes swirling around them. Ross flipped up the collar of his suit and held it close. He scanned the street right and left but did not see the Audi or Inus.

"Do you see him?" asked Lin.

Craning his neck to the left and right, Ross said, "No I don't. I don't see him at all."

Suddenly Ross had a sinking feeling. He reached into his pants pocket and pulled out the business card Inus had given him.

"I've got a bad feeling about this," said Ross as he punched up Inus's phone number on his Samsung.

Inus's phone was ringing but he wasn't picking up.

"Come on, pick up," said Ross.

Then Inus answered the phone.

"Hello James," said Inus.

"Where are you Lon? I don't see you out front," said Ross.

"James, this is one I'm doing by myself," said Inus.

Ross looked at Lin.

"No! We do this together. We stick with the plan," said Ross.

"This always was the plan, James," said Inus.

"No!" said Ross.

"Listen to me James. You and Lin have the rest of your lives together. You have a beautiful future. I can tell," said Inus.

"Wait a minute …" pleaded Ross.

"It has to be this way James. My life is all behind me, yours is all in front. I beg you, let me do this alone. I've been doing it for a long time. Maybe he'll even have mercy on me tonight."

"Who?" asked Ross. "Who will have mercy?"

"I think you know James," said Inus.

Lin motioned for Ross to give her the phone.

"Longinus this is Lin."

"Ah Lin. Sweet, gentle Lin. You have many special gifts. You have a good man there. Take care of him," said Inus.

"Let us help you," said Lin. "We can do this together."

"I've got to go now Lin. I'll remember you both. Love each other, and may God bless you always."

Then Inus hung up.

Ross was already running over to the valet station.

He pulled the ticket out of his wallet and gave it to the young man.

"I need my car quickly," said Ross. "It's a black Mercedes-Benz."

The young man said, “Yes sir right away.” He grabbed the ticket and sprinted into the garage. In two minutes the Mercedes-Benz was screeching to a halt in front of the valet station.

“Here you are sir,” said the young valet handing Ross his keys.

Ross and Lin jumped into the Mercedes and sped away into the night.

Inus followed the GPS coordinates Lin had given for her location just hours before.

*God’s will be done,* he prayed.

He pulled into the Burggarten and parked his Audi.

*Lord strengthen my arm.*

His 1940 Eterna chronograph told him it was 2132 hours.

*Let not mine enemies triumph over me.*

Inus noticed three BMW sedans parked in the same lot.

*No one should be parked here at night,* he thought.

Inus got out of the Audi. He glanced skyward. Glistening snowflakes where softly floating down in the dark, illuminated by a full moon and the single iridescent lamp post high overhead.

“Such a beautiful night,” he said.

Then he hunched up his shoulders against the cold and walked towards the BMWs.

Almost simultaneously, Nü Jiangshi, Ming Chen, and Chong Zee exited each of the BMWs and walked forward. Ming and Chong were carrying AK-47 assault rifles.

Inus stopped about twenty feet in front of the Chinese. The scene was reminiscent of an old *film noir* gunfight.

“Good evening Mister Inus,” said Nü invitingly.

Inus was surprised.

“You know who I am?” he asked.

“I know your name,” replied Nü. “Whether it is your real name or not I will find out soon enough. I did some checking on you today after seeing you with Captain Ross at the museum. You are actually quite a mystery.”

“I see,” said Inus. “Did you bring the spear?”

“Yes, here it is,” said Nü. She reached inside her overcoat and pulled out the Spear of Destiny.

The gold ornamentation of the spear was glittering in the moonlight.

“It really is quite beautiful,” said Nü.

“Let me see it,” said Inus.

“Can you imagine,” said Nü, “that a Roman Centurian actually stabbed Jesus Christ with this spear …”

“Let me have it,” demanded Inus.

“… over two thousand years ago?”

“Give me the spear!” yelled Inus.

Nü cast a quick glance at each of her comrades and then slowly walked forward. She stopped about three feet in front of Inus and then dropped the spear to the ground.

*Stupid woman,* thought Inus. *Stupid, stupid woman.*

Inus took a step forward and picked up the spear. He wiped off the snow and held the blade up to the moonlight.

He examined the wire that was used to bind the nail to the spear.

*Yes, this is the one,* he thought. *This is my spear.*

"Satisfied?" asked Nü.

"Yes, yes I am," replied Inus.

"Well then, as you can see, we have fulfilled our end of the deal," said Nü.

The vampire took a step closer.

Inus could smell her perfume.

"Angels' Share by Kilian Paris," said Inus.

Nü was surprised.

"Why yes, that's right," she said.

"So you know your perfumes. Now, where is Die Glocke?"

"I'm afraid I've changed the terms of our deal," said Inus. "There is no Die Glocke. There never was. So, I take the spear back and return it to the Hofburg, and you simply go home."

Nü leaned in close.

"Give me Die Glocke now, or I will kill you and take back the spear and still find Die Glocke."

Nü sneered at Inus.

"You are all alone here, abandoned by your friends."

At that moment the Mercedes with Ross and Lin roared into the parking lot.

Nü and her two Chinese teammates turned to see the Mercedes screech to a halt behind them. The headlights momentarily blinded the Chinese and they raised their hands to shield their eyes.

"The American!" screamed Ming.

Ross left the Mercedes lights on as he and Lin got out of the car. They crouched behind the open doors using them for cover. Then Ross leveled his Beretta at the Chinese.

Inus smiled.

"Not quite alone," he said.

*RAT-A-TAT-TAT!*

*RAT-A-TAT-TAT!*

*RAT-A-TAT-TAT!*

The Chinese opened fire with their AK-47 assault rifles. 7.62x39mm bullets were whizzing through the night like angry wasps, smacking into the Mercedes and kicking up snow.

Ross returned fire with the Beretta.

*KA-POW!*

*KA-POW!*

Nü turned around to see Inus drawing out his pistol. Her years of Wushu martial arts training kicked in and she automatically knocked his gun arm away with one hand while twisting at the waist to deliver a quick sweeping kick knocking his legs out from under him.

Inus fell hard on his back but kept a hold of the spear.

Nü was bending over and reaching down to grab the spear when Inus drew both knees to his chest and lashed out with a devastating doubled-footed kick to Nü's face.

Nü was knocked backwards head over heals and lay spread eagled in the snow.

Inus rolled over to his feet and yelled, "Mozart, head for Mozart!"

Ross yelled to Lin, "Keep low and run to the Mozart statue!"

Ross and Lin made a desperate dash for the monument.

Chong Zee arched his arm back and looked like he was throwing a rock at their car.

*KA-BOOM!*

No sooner had Ross and Lin left the safety of the Mercedes than the entire car was engulfed in flames.

It wasn't a rock. It was a thermite incendiary grenade.

Searing golden flames rising from the Mercedes licked and swooned at the night sky reminiscent of a macabre scene from Dante's Inferno.

Inus made it to the statue first.

"Come on!" yelled Inus to Ross and Lin. "Come on!"

Inus led his friends to the rear concrete base of the Mozart statue. There he hurriedly wiped the snow off of a panel revealing a metal handle. He placed both hands on the frozen handle and pulled with all his might. The hinges let out a hideous screech and then the panel opened.

"Quick, follow me," said Inus.

They all turned on their cellphone flashlights with Inus leading the way.

They walked down frozen concrete steps which led into an ancient tunnel complex built as a bomb shelter over a hundred years ago during the First World War.

Deeper and deeper, step by step, down and down they went.

Lin brushed the endless cobwebs away from her face as she followed Ross and Inus deeper into the dank, musty tunnel.

Ross noticed several passageways at intervals leading off to the right and left.

"Where do those passageways go?" asked Ross.

"To ammunition storage bunkers," said Inus.

"Where are we going to come out at?" asked Ross.

"This particular tunnel will lead us right into an ancient burial crypt beneath the Hofburg Palace," said Inus.

"Beneath the palace?" asked Ross incredulously, swiping cobwebs out of his hair.

"Yes," replied Inus. "Most of Vienna is interconnected underground by a vast array of tunnels, catacombs, and vaults. The oldest ones date back to ancient Roman times."

"Here we are," said Inus.

They came face-to-face with two huge rustic oak doors which looked to be several hundred years old. Inus took a hold of the double wrought iron handles and pulled. The double doors creaked open in the middle and Ross helped push one to the side.

Inus stepped inside and flicked on a light switch. A bank of overhead florescent lights flickered to life.

The crypt was huge, at least two thousand square feet. It had a stone floor and stone walls. Huge tapestries depicting Victorian scenes hung from the walls. In the middle of the room plush Victorian red leather parlor chairs surrounded a large lacquered oak table. On the table was a bust of Napoleon Bonaparte. Against the walls were multiple sarcophagi containing the mortal remains of princes, generals, noblemen and their ladies. A large bar was set at the far side wall with a well stocked liquor cabinet.

"Have you been here before Longinus?" asked Lin.

Inus turned to Lin and smiled.

"Yes. I helped build this," said Inus, "long ago."

Ross saw flashes of light coming from the tunnel behind them.

"I think we've got company," said Ross. "Is there a way out of here?"

Inus pointed to the liquor cabinet.

"Over here."

Inus went behind the bar and flipped a switch. The liquor cabinet rumbled slightly then slid away to reveal a secret staircase.

"Let's go," said Inus.

With Inus in the lead the trio climbed the spiral metal staircase.

"This takes us to the chapel," said Inus.

Twisting and turning up the metal steps to the first floor, the staircase opened into a dressing room behind the sanctuary.

Inus led them through the dressing room and into the sanctuary as footsteps were heard rapidly *click-clacking* up the staircase.

The chapel was richly illuminated by the flickering flames of several ceiling and wall mounted candelabras. An extravagant alter was adored with multiple golden statues of the Holy Family and the apostles. An oblong table in front of the altar was covered with a white silk cloth on which rested a huge black leather-bound Latin bible and three upright golden crucifixes.

Ross turned and could hear the hurried footsteps climbing the staircase.

"Take cover behind the pews," said Ross.

No sooner had Ross said this than the three Chinese agents burst into the chapel with guns blazing.

*RAT-A-TAT-TAT!*

*RAT-A-TAT-TAT!*

Fully automatic AK-47 assault rifles bucked in the hands of Ming and Chong as they fired around the chapel.

Ross, Lin, and Inus ducked behind a mahogany pew for cover.

7.62mm bullets were taking chunks out of the stone chapel walls. Then Nü Jiangshi entered the chapel and stood defiantly between her colleagues.

"Captain Ross," said Nü, "you and your comrades have put up a valiant struggle, but it is over now."

The vampire's voice was echoing off the chapel walls.

Ross was reloading his Beretta behind the church pew and listening.

"I think you can appreciate this place of worship. You and your comrades are Christian, no? In consideration of this place, I will allow Miss Sparrow to leave unharmed, I promise you. That is, if you cooperate. All I want is you, your friend, and the spear. And I promise you a swift execution, if you surrender now!" yelled Nü.

Ross gave the Beretta to Lin.

"Here take this." Ross pressed the Beretta into Lin's hand. "They won't promise you any safe passage, believe me. But they'll have to kill us before they get to you," said Ross.

Inus pulled out the Chinese pistol and slid it across the wooden bench seat to Ross.

"None of us die today," said Inus.

Then Inus stood up with his hands in the air. In his right hand he held the Spear of Destiny.

"All right," said Inus, "all right."

Inus started slowly walking down the pew. He turned to walk into the center aisle. Then he stopped.

"I've got what you want," said Inus, "right here."

Nü Jiangshi — the vampire — the walking corpse — was pleased with herself.

"Come closer," she smiled and motioned to Inus with her hand.

Nü nodded her head to Chong who had a fragmentation grenade in his pocket.

*I've got this bastard now,* thought Nü. *I'll kill him and get the spear, then we'll finish off the American and his whore girlfriend.*

"Come," said Nü beckoning to Inus.

# *CHAPTER NINETEEN*

# *WALKING CORPSE*

Inus slowly walked forward down the church aisle with both hands over his head, holding the spear. He stopped about two feet in front of Nü and lowered his hands offering the spear to her.

"Here it is," said Inus.

Nü smiled at him and held out her hand.

Ross and Lin watched as the scene unfolded.

*What the hell is he gonna do?* thought Ross.

"Why do you seek the Longinus Spear?" asked Inus.

Nü Jiangshi — the walking corpse — the vampire — who had turned over her own parents to a communist concentration camp, who had betrayed every friend she ever had, who had risen through the ranks on greed, power, deceit, and treachery, looked at Inus with curiosity.

"I could care less about the spear," said Nü. "It means nothing to me except as a symbol of how pathetically weak your country has become. To me it symbolizes your belief in superstitious religions, false gods, and stupidity."

Inus thrust the spear forward. Nü doubled over as the Holy Lance pierced her stomach and embedded in her liver. Sanguineous vermillion blood oozed down the blade and shaft. She reached up trying to grab Longinus by the throat, but only succeeded in scratching his face with her fingernails.

"Bastard Christian," gasped Nü between clenched teeth.

"That's me," replied Inus.

Ming and Chong swung their rifles around to blast Inus in half, but Ross had other plans.

*KA-POW!*

*KA-POW!*

Ross placed a bullet into each of the Chinese assassin's heads. They collapsed to the chapel floor amongst the clatter of their rifles.

Lin and Ross ran up the aisle to Inus.

"Are you Okay?" asked Ross.

Inus turned to him and said, "Yes, and thank you my friend." Looking at the dead Chinese assassins, Inus said, "I had no idea you were such a good shot."

Lin knelt down over Nü.

"Oh my God," said Lin.

In the flash of an instant Nü's eyes blinked open and she reached up. She grabbed Lin by the throat with one hand and pulled the Spear of Destiny out of her own stomach with the other. Nü was ready to strike when Lin suddenly pulled out her SS dagger and plunged it into Nü's heart until it impaled her to the floor.

Inus and Ross watched in amazement.

Ross stretched out his hand and helped Lin to her feet.

"That's how you kill a vampire," said Ross.

Inus leaned over and pulled the SS dagger out of Nü Jiangshi. He wiped the blade back and forth on her jacket to clean off the blood.

"Here you go Lin," said Inus handing her back the dagger. Noticing that it was a Nazi-era Schutzstaffel dagger, Inus said, "Strange choice for a weapon."

Ross picked up the Spear of Destiny from the floor and handed it to Inus, who walked over to the altar table. He grabbed an altar linen cloth and wrote *ORIGINAL LONGINUS SPEAR* on it for the Hofburg staff. Then he reverently placed the spear on top of it and placed a golden crucifix on either side.

"Let's get out of here," said Inus.

The three friends went through the chapel and back down the spiral staircase.

"Why didn't any alarms go off?" asked Ross.

Inus said, "Because the staff turned them off as a courtesy gesture for the Chinese Archeology Team's review. They didn't want to offend."

They retraced their steps through the burial crypt and entered the tunnels. Ross looked at his Benrus and saw it was midnight.

Inus led them through the tunnels and back to the Mozart monument.

Several Bundespolizei sedans with flashing red lights were pulled up behind the smoldering hulk of Ross's Mercedes-Benz. Officers were encircling it and in the process of squelching the fire with portable fire extinguishers. The three BMW sedans of the Chinese team were parked about twenty yards in front of the Mercedes. Inus's Audi A5 Cabriolet was still where he had left it, about thirty yards to the front.

Inus, Ross and Lin were crouched behind the base of the Mozart monument and observed the scene.

"I'm sorry about your car," whispered Inus.

Ross nodded.

"I don't think we should chance trying to get to my car. It would attract too much attention," said Inus.

Ross scanned up and down the parking lot.

"Yeah, it would be impossible," he said.

"Okay," said Inus. "Follow me and keep low."

Inus led Ross and Lin from the Mozart monument to the far side of the Burggarten. They walked through several gardens and past multiple monuments until they came upon another parking lot with a sign proclaiming *AUSGANG*.

"There's the exit sign," said Inus.

The three friends walked out of the Burggarten and continued towards the Kohlmarket and the Graben shopping area, which was brightly illuminated everywhere with red and green twinkling Christmas lights. Ross was surprised that the merchant shops were still open after midnight.

Shop windows were warmly illuminated displaying the latest designer fashions and tourist gifts. Ornately decorated horse-drawn carriages with blanket covered couples were clip-clopping along on every street. Soon they came upon the steam covered window of a French restaurant named Le Bol.

Inus stopped in his tracks and smiled at Ross.

"Are you thinking what I'm thinking?" said Inus.

Ross grinned and offered his forearm to Lin.

"Shall we?" he asked.

Lin slipped her arm around his and said, "There's nothing I'd like better right now than a nice hot bowl of French onion soup."

# *CHAPTER TWENTY*

# *TIMELESS DESTINY*

The three friends enjoyed French onion soup and rum at Le Bol until just after one in the morning. They reminisced about what just happened, and talked about the future.

Inus took off his suit coat jacket and hung it on the back of his chair. He casually rolled up the sleeves of his shirt to the elbows. Ross immediately noticed the SPQR tattoo on his left forearm.

"Interesting tattoo," said Ross. "Your old unit?"

Inus looked at his arm.

"Yes," he said. "Some things die hard."

Seeing a change of subject was needed, Lin said, "I sure didn't expect to get into a gunfight in a burial crypt under the Hofburg tonight."

Inus and Ross laughed.

"Yeah," said Ross, "quite unexpected."

"And this vampire lady was quite formidable," said Inus.

Lin nodded.

"She surprised me at the end, that's for sure," said Lin.

"I don't think I will ever forget the image of you plunging your German dagger into her," said Inus. "That was unforeseen. Tell me, why do you carry an SS dagger?"

Ross chimed in, "I can answer that. You see, the original Die Glocke shifter lever, sort of like a gearshift handle on a car, broke off. So, I had to come up with a field expedient replacement."

Inus chuckled, "And you just happened to have an SS danger lying around?"

Ross laughed. "Um, I took it off the desk of the Nazi who was in league with radical Islamic terrorists."

Inus said, "That's certainly a bad combination."

"The Chinese were pretty brazen to attempt an attack on the spear and another on Die Glocke, weren't they?" said Ross.

Lin said, "And at the same time too."

"I'm afraid," said Inus, "that they will become more brazen. Everything in the world today seems to be upside down. All we can do is remain vigilant and continue standing up for freedom."

Ross said, "So Lon, what will you do now?"

Inus poured some Coca-Cola in with his rum and stirred.

"I shall continue with my life here, protecting the spear, and waiting."

According to legend, Longinus had to wait until Christ returned to the earth before he would know peace.

"But I can tell you, I will miss the both of you, my new friends," said Inus. Then he raised his glass in a toast.

"To James and Lin," said Inus. "May God bless you and keep you always, and may blue skies and calm seas follow you all the days of your life."

Ross and Lin raised their glasses and *clinked* them with Inus.

"Thank you Lon," said Ross.

Lin leaned over and kissed Inus on the cheek. "Thank you."

Inus touched his cheek.

"Oh my," said Inus, "I'm afraid I'm just not used to such kindness."

The waiter brought the check and Inus took it.

"Hey," said Ross, "let me get that."

Inus shook his head.

"No, no my friend," said Inus. "It is my pleasure."

Inus paid the bill while Ross and Lin finished their drinks.

"Ready?" asked Inus.

The three friends left Le Bol Restaurant and walked out into the brisk night.

They strolled down Kaertnerstrasse to Herrengasse, and soon they were in front of the Herrenhof Steigenberger Hotel.

"I guess this is it," said Inus.

Ross nodded.

"Is there anything you need?" asked Inus.

"Not really. It's been fun," said Ross. He reached out his hand to Inus.

Inus shook hands with Ross and said, "Until that time my friend, until that time."

Lin walked to Inus and gave him a big hug.

"Thank you for everything," she said.

Inus pointed to the Steigenberger.

"You know, there's a nice little lounge right in there. It's very quaint, and has a nice atmosphere. And couples dance."

"Really?" asked Lin.

Inus said, "Or so I've heard."

Ross said, "Lin's been trying to get me to dance for a long time."

Inus shrugged his shoulders.

"You see? Give it a try," he said.

# *EPILOGUE*

*The bravest are surely those who have the clearest vision of what is before them, glory and danger alike, and yet notwithstanding, go out to meet it.*

Thucydides
460 — 400 BC
Athenian General

# *TIME STARTS NOW*

Lin walked out of the ladies room and into the dark noisy lounge.

Watching the couples joining and becoming one on the dance floor, she peered through the smoky air, searching for Ross.

I *can feel James here,* she thought.

Then she sees him, sitting at a far corner table, alone, waiting.

Trying hard to control her heart, she walks over to him.

There they meet, softly, gently, reassuringly.

"Hello Mister," says Lin.

Teasingly she asks, "Are you waiting for anyone?"

Ross stands up.

"Yes I am.  I'm waiting for my love," he says.

"Here," says Lin taking his hand, "let me show you where it is."

They move to the dance floor and embrace.

Two hearts become one as they start swaying to the music.

Slowly at first, ever slowly.

They look deeply into each others eyes.

"What are you thinking about Lin?" asks Ross.

"Us," she replies.

"What are you thinking about Jamie?"

"You," replied Ross.

Then he leans in and they kiss.

Soon time stands still.

Longinus was standing outside, peering into the lounge's large picturesque window. He observed the entire scene.

Flipping up his collar to the cold, he looked skyward and said, "Thank you."

Then he smiled.

Longinus walked slowly away, and was soon lost to view in the darkness and the gently swirling snow.

**THE END**

# ABOUT THE AUTHOR

Bernard Cenney retired from the United States Army as a Lieutenant Colonel after more than twenty-eight years in uniform. He considers it a privilege to have served his country throughout numerous command and staff assignments the world over. He makes Texas his home.

www.ingramcontent.com/pod-product-compliance
Lightning Source LLC
Chambersburg PA
CBHW030423310726
48979CB00009B/1595/J
* 9 7 8 1 7 3 6 2 4 5 1 9 4 *